Paul Leicester Ford

Tattle-tales of Cupid

Paul Leicester Ford

Tattle-tales of Cupid

ISBN/EAN: 9783742894373

Manufactured in Europe, USA, Canada, Australia, Japa

Cover: Foto ©Andreas Hilbeck / pixelio.de

Manufactured and distributed by brebook publishing software
(www.brebook.com)

Paul Leicester Ford

Tattle-tales of Cupid

TATTLE-TALES

OF

CUPID

TOLD BY

PAUL LEICESTER FORD

NEW YORK

DODD, MEAD AND COMPANY

1898

TO MY PLAYMATE

My dear Doña :

Once upon a time two children read aloud together more or less of *Darwin, Spencer, Lyell, Goethe, Carlyle, Taine,* and other writers of equal note. Though the books were somewhat above their comprehension, and certainly not so well suited to their years as fairy-tales and romances, both the choice and the rejection were deliberately made and consistently maintained. The discrimination originated neither in excessive fondness of fact, nor in the slightest dislike of fiction; being solely due to a greater preference for the stories they themselves created than for those they found in books. Presently, one of these two, having found a new playfellow, stopped inventing and acting and living their joint imaginings, and the other one had to go on playing by himself. But he has never forgotten the original impulse, and so, in collecting the offspring of some of his earliest and some of his latest play-hours, his

*thoughts recur to the years of the old partnership, and
he cannot please himself better than by putting his
playmate, where she truly belongs, at the beginning of
his " imaginary " playthings.*

NOTE

"His Version of It" is reprinted in this form by permission of the Century Company.

"The Cortelyou Feud" is reprinted by permission of Messrs. Harper and Brothers.

Contents

HIS VERSION OF IT

Tattle-Tales of Cupid

HIS VERSION OF IT

"SHE's a darling!" exclaimed the bay mare, between munches of the big red apple.

"That's just what she is!" responded the off carriage-horse; and then, as part of his apple fell to the floor, he added fretfully: "I do wish, Lassie, that you girls wouldn't talk to a fellow when he's doing something! You've made me lose half my apple!"

Old Reveille, with the prudence of twenty-eight years of experience, carefully deposited the unmasticated fraction of his apple beside an uneaten one in his manger before remarking reflectively: "She's a thoroughbred; but she's not the beauty her mother was at the same age."

" Fie ! " reproved one of the cobs: " how can you be so ungallant, when she always gives you an extra apple or piece of sugar ? "

" I call it shameful unfairness," growled the nigh horse of the pair. " She does n't keep you up till two or three in the morning at balls and cotillions. She does n't so much as ride you in the park, as she does Lassie or Bubbles. When you have n't done a step of work in six years, and spend your summers out in the pasture and your winters in a box-stall eating your head off, why should you get a double portion ? "

" Yes," whinnied Bubbles, plaintively; "and, what 's more, she always kisses you."

Reveille, who meantime had swallowed his first apple, looked up with a lofty smile of superiority. Then he slowly winked his off eye, remarked, " Naturally, you don't understand it," and fell to lipping his second apple caressingly, previous to the decisive crunch. " See if that does n't drive the women wild," he cogitated, with a grin.

" Now is n't that just like a man ! " complained Lassie. " As if it was n't enough to get more than his share, but he must go and have a secret along with it."

" Huh ! " grunted the polo pony, who was, of necessity, the brains-carrier of the stable; " if it 's family property, it can't be much of a secret; for I never heard of anything to which six humans were privy that did n't at once become town gossip. And they must be aware of it, for, from the Major to the Minor, they discriminate in favor of Reveille in a manner most reprehensible." The polo pony was famous for the choiceness of his language and the neatness of his wit; but he was slightly vain, as was shown by his adding : " Pretty good, that, eh ? Major — that 's the man we take out riding or driving. Minor — that 's the three-year-old. Do you hitch up to that post ? "

" Do they all know your secret, Reveille ? " asked Lassie, ingratiatingly.

" They think they do," replied the veteran. " They don't, though," he added; and then, heaving a sigh, he continued : " But the roan filly did, and Mr. Lewis's big grey, and dear old Sagitta — that was the Russian wolf-hound, who died before any of you youngsters joined our set."

" Then I fail to perceive," remarked the polo pony, " why they should treat you differently, if they are ignorant of the circumstances to which you refer."

" My dear colt," retorted Reveille, " when you are grown to horsehood you will learn that we are all governed by our imaginations, and not by our knowledge. Why do you shy at a scrap of white paper? Superficially because you are nearly related to an ass, actually because your fancy makes it into a white elephant."

" And how about your putting your head and tail up, and careering all over the home lot, last summer, just because our Major fired his revolver at a hawk? Were you an ass, too ? " saucily questioned one of the cobs.

"Probably," assented the oldster, genially; "for that very incident proves my
point. What that shot reminded me of
was the last time I heard my Major fire
his revolver. I saw a long, gentle slope,
up which a brigade of 'secesh' were
charging to a railroad embankment pro-
tected by a battery of twelve-pounders fir-
ing six rounds of case-shot to the minute.
And I was right among the guns again,
seeing and hearing it all; and my Major
— only he was a captain then — was
saying as coolly and quietly as he orders
the carriage now: 'Steady, men, steady!
There's a hundred yards yet, and they
can't stand it to the finish. Double
charge with canister! Three more rounds
will settle them.' Which was just what it
did. We horses, with the aid of the men
and guns, held the Weldon railroad,
and Lee and his mules stopped holding
Richmond."

"Doesn't he tell a story beautifully?"
remarked Bubbles, in a distinctly audible
aside to Lassie.

"I've never known a better raconteur," answered Lassie, in a stage whisper of equal volume.

"Lay you a peck of oats to a quart that the girls get that secret out of him," whispered the Major's saddle-horse, who, as a Kentuckian of thoroughbred stock, had sporting and race-track proclivities.

"Not with me!" denied the second cob. "Besides, no gentleman ever bets on a certainty. Gaze at the self-satisfied look on the old fool's phiz. Lord! how a pretty face and figure, combined with flattery, can come it round the old ones!"

There could be no doubt about it. Reveille was smirking, though trying not to desperately; and to aid his attempt, he went on, with a pretence of unconscious musing, as if he were still in the past: "Yes; we are ruled by our imaginations, and, consequently, though I have reached the honourable but usually neglected period in life which retires an officer and a horse from active service, I get a box-stall and extra rations and perquisites."

"How rarely is the story-telling faculty united with the philosophical mind!" soliloquised Bubbles to the rafters.

"And how rarely," rejoined Lassie, "are those two qualities combined with a finished, yet graphic, style!"

"I would gladly tell you that story," said the old war-horse, "but it isn't one to be repeated. Every horse who isn't a cow — to make an Irish bull, which, by the bye, is a very donkeyish form of joke — has done certain things that he has keenly regretted, even though he believes that he acted for the good — just as brave soldiers will act as spies, honourable lawyers defend a scoundrel, and good women give 'at homes.'"

"What a decadence there has been in true wit!" remarked Lassie, apropos of nothing. "It is such a pleasure to be put next a horse at dinner whose idea of humour was formed before youthful pertness was allowed to masquerade as wit."

"It is a mortification to me to this day," went on Reveille, "even though the outcome has justified me. You know what our equine code of honour is — how we won't lie or trick or steal or kill, as the humans do. Well, for nearly two months I was as false and tricky as a man."

"I don't believe it," dissented Bubbles.

"The truly great always depreciate themselves," asserted one of the mares.

"No, ladies, I speak the truth," reiterated the warrior; "even now the memory galls me worse than a spur."

"It would ease your conscience, I am sure," suggested Bubbles, "to confess the wrong, if wrong there was. A highly sensitive and chivalric nature so often takes a morbidly extreme view of what is at most but a peccadillo."

"This, alas! was no peccadillo," sighed Reveille, "as you will acknowledge after hearing it."

"I may be a colt, but I'm not a dolt," sneered the polo pony to himself. "As if we weren't all aware that the garrulous old fool has been itching to inflict his long tail upon us for the last ten minutes."

"My one consolation," continued Reveille, "is that the roan filly was in the
traces with me and an equal culprit in —"

"I thought that one of the sex of Adam
would saddle it on a woman before he got
through," interjected the cob.

"*Cherchez la femme!*" laughed the polo
pony, delighted to trot out his French.

"All I meant to suggest, ladies and
gentlemen," affirmed Reveille, reflectively,
"is that a woman is an excuse for anything. If this world is a fine world, it is
because she pulls the reins more often for
good than for bad."

"'Those who always praise woman
know her but little; those who always
blame her know her not at all,'" quoted
the worldly-wise Kentuckian.

Reveille swallowed the last fragment of
his second apple, cleared his throat, and
began : —

"It was after Five Forks, where my
Captain got a major's oak-leaf added to
his shoulder-straps, and a Minié ball in
his arm, that the thing began. When he

came out of the hospital — long before he should have, for the bone had been shattered, and took its own time to knit — we hung about Washington, swearing at our bad luck, my Major suffering worse than a docked horse in fly-time from the little splinters of bone that kept working out, and I eating my head off in — "

" History does repeat itself," murmured the envious carriage-horse.

" Well, one day, after nearly three months of idleness, when I was about dead with stalldom, I permitted the orderly to saddle me, and after a little dispute with him as to my preferences, I let him take me round to Scott Square. There for the first time I met the roan filly and the big grey. She was a dear ! " he added, with a sigh, and paused a moment.

" Ah, don't stop there ! " begged one of the ladies.

" Get a gait on you," exhorted the cob.

Reveille sighed again softly, shook his head, and then came back to the present.

" ' May you never lack for oats and

grass,' said I, greeting them in my most affable style.

" ' May you die in clover,' responded the grey, nodding politely.

" ' May you have all the sugar you desire,' added the filly, sweetly, and greeting me with a graceful toss of the head. That told me that a woman belonged to her, for men never give sugar. Sometimes, on a forced march, my Major used to divide his ration of hardtack with me; but I never tasted sugar until — well, we must n't get ahead too fast."

" No danger, while he is doing the lipping," grumbled the disagreeable cob.

" ' I see by your saddle that you are in the service,' remarked the big grey. ' I am not so fortunate. Between ourselves, I think the fellow I let ride me would do anything sooner than fight — though, now it 's all over, he says if he 'd returned from Europe in time he should have gone into the army.'

" I shook my head dejectedly. ' I 'm very much off my feed,' I told them. ' My Major is not able to ride, and won't be for a long time, so I'm horribly afraid I've been sold. I really would n't have believed it of him!'

"'What things man is capable of doing!' sighed the filly, with tears of sympathy in her eyes.

"'Cheer up, comrade,' cried the grey, consolingly. 'Even if you are sold, you might be worse off. You are still a saddle-horse, and as Miss Gaiety and I both have good stables, you probably will have the same luck, since you are in our set. The fellow I carry spurred my predecessor, when he was leg weary, at an impossible jump in Leicestershire, and because he fell short and spoiled his knees the brute ordered him sold, and he was put to dragging a huckster's cart, besides being half starved. You're not so bad off as that yet.'

"Just then three people came out of the house before which we were standing, and I can't tell you how my heart jumped with joy, and how my ears went forward, when I saw that one of them was my Major. For the instant I was so happy that I felt like kicking up; but the next moment I was ready to die with mortification at the thought of how I had cheapened him to strangers.   Think of my saying such things to them of the best man that ever lived!

"'That's *my Major*,' I told them, arching my neck and flicking my tail with pride. 'He held the Weldon railroad without—'"

"But you told us a little while ago," protested Lassie, "that—"

"Yes, yes," hastily broke in the story-teller with a note of deprecation in his voice. "Don't you see, girls, that having just belittled him, I had to give him the credit of it, though really we horses— But there, I won't go into that now."

"That much is saved!" muttered the cob.

"Walpole," said the polo pony, "well described a certain period of life when he denied that a man was in his dotage, but suggested that he was in his 'anecdotage.'"

"It was far from my intention—" Reveille began, with dignity.

"I do wish you would bridle your tongues, the two of you," snapped Bubbles. "It's just what I should expect of a colt that has never seen anything better than a poplar ball and a wooden mallet, and so dislikes to hear of real battles. Please pay no heed to him, Mr. Reveille."

"We don't notice either of them one curb or snaffle bit," declared Lassie, "so why should you? Forgive me for interrupting you, and do tell us what you told the steeds about our Major?"

Reveille hesitated, and then resumed his tale: "'His battery held the Weldon railroad without any infantry supports,' I told them, adding, 'Sheridan's right-hand man. Perfect devil at fighting, and the kindest human in the world.'

"The roan filly, being a woman, answered: 'He looks both;' but the grey, being something more stupid, remarked: 'Then what made you think he had sold you?'

"'Dear Mr. Solitaire,' cried the mare, 'you must know that we all say things in society, not because we think them, but to make conversation. I knew Mr. — thank you, Mr. Reveille — was joking the moment he spoke.' I tell you, gentlemen, women can put the blinders on facts when they really try!

" 'What do you think of my Felicia?' asked Miss Gaiety.

" I had been so taken up with my dear that I had n't so much as looked at hers. But, oh, fellows, she was a beauty! Filly built, right through — just made to be shown off by a habit; hair as smooth as a mare's coat, and as long and thick as an undocked tail; eyes — oh, well, halter it! there is no use trying to describe her eyes, or her nose, or her mouth, or her smile. She was just the dearest, loveliest darling that I ever did see!

" Mr. Lewis was putting her up, while my poor dear stood watching them, with a look in his face I had never seen. Now, when there was anything to be done, my Major was always the man who did it, and it puzzled me why he had let Mr. Lewis get

the better of him. The next instant I saw
that his right arm was still in a sling, and
that his sword-sash was used to tie it to
his body. Then I knew why he had an
up-and-down line in his forehead, and why
he bit his mustache.

"'Can I give you any help, Major
Moran?' asked Mr. Lewis, when he had
helped Miss Fairley mount.

"'Thanks, no,' answered my pal, rather
curtly, I thought; and putting his left
hand on me, into the saddle he vaulted.
But he was foolish to do it, as he said
'Ouch!' below his breath; and he must
have turned pale, for Miss Fairley cried out,
'Mr. Lewis, quick! He's going to faint!'

"'Nothing of the kind,' denied my
backer, giving a good imitation laugh,
even while his hand gripped my neck and
I felt him swerve in the saddle. 'Miss
Fairley, I will not let even you keep me
an interesting invalid. If there was any
fighting left, I should long since have
been ordered to the front by the surgeons;
but now they wink their eyes at shirking.'

" ' I told you you ought not to go, and now I 'm sure of it,' urged Miss Fairley. 'You 'll never be able to control such a superb and spirited horse with only your left arm.' "

" Bet that 's a subsequent piece of embroidery," whispered the polo pony to his nearest neighbor.

" Now, I have to confess that I had come out of the stable feeling full of friskiness, and I had n't by any means worked it off on the orderly, much of a dance as I 'd given him. But the way I put a check-strap on my spirits and dropped my tail and ears and head was a circumstance, I tell you.

" ' There 's not the slightest cause for alarm,' my confrère answered her. ' The old scamp has an inclination to lose his head in battle, but he 's steady enough as a roadster.'

" ' I really wish, though, that you would n't insist on coming,' persisted Miss Fairley, anxiously. ' You know — '

" ' Of course, Miss Fairley,' interrupted

my Major, with a nasty little laugh, 'if
you prefer to have your ride a solitude *à
deux*, and I am in —'

"'Shall we start?' interrupted Miss
Fairley, her cheeks very red, and her eyes
blazing. She didn't wait for an answer,
but touched up the filly into a trot, and
for the first mile or two not a word would
she say to my colleague; and even when
he finally got her to answer him, she
showed that she wasn't going to forget
that speech.

"Well, what began like this went from
bad to worse. He wasn't even aware that
he had been shockingly rude, and never
so much as apologised for his speech.
When Miss Fairley didn't ask him to ride
with them the next day, he ordered me
saddled, and joined them on the road;
and this he did again and again, though
she was dreadfully cool to him. My dear
seemed unable to behave. He couldn't
be himself. He was rude to Mr. Lewis,
sulky to Miss Fairley, and kept a dreadful
rein on me. That week was the only time

in my life when he rode me steadily on the curb. My grief! how my jaw did ache!"

"I wish it would now," interrupted the cob, sulkily. Let it be said here that horses are remarkably sweet-natured but this particular one was developing a splint, and was inevitably cross.

"Don't be a nag," requested one of the mares.

"The roan filly always blamed my Major for making such a mess of the whole thing; but even though I recognised how foolish he was to kick over the traces, I saw there were reasons enough to excuse him. In the first place, he enlisted when he was only nineteen, and having served straight through, he had had almost no experience of women. Then for six months he had been suffering terribly with his arm, with the result that what was left of his nerves were all on edge. He began to ride before he ought, and though I did my best to be easy, I suppose that every moment in the saddle must have caused him intense pain.

Finally, he had entered himself for the running only after Mr. Lewis had turned the first mile-post and had secured the inside track. I really think, if ever a man was justified in fretting on the bit my chum was.

"At the end of the week Miss Gaiety bade me good-bye. 'I heard Mr. Fairley say that we could now go back to Yantic; that's where we live, you know,' she told me. 'It's been a long job getting our claim for uniforms and blankets allowed, but the controller signed a warrant yesterday. I'm really sorry that we are to be separated. If your associate had behaved decently, you might have been asked to visit us.'

"'Yes,' announced the big grey; 'Miss Fairley has asked the bully who rides me and myself to spend a few days with you next week. I suppose they'll settle it then.'

"But the officer and horse who commanded the battery which held the Weldon railroad weren't going to be beaten as easily as that, you may be sure! When I took my rider back to the stable that

afternoon, I heard him say to the orderly:
'Jackson, I'm going north next week, and
shall want Reveille to start before me.
I'm in too much pain to give you your
orders now, but come round to-morrow
morning and get your instructions.'

"Yantic was nothing but a little village
clustered about a great woollen-mill, without any stable or hotel to live in, so we
had to put up at Norwich, a place seven
miles away; and it was a case of put up,
I tell you, in both food and attendance!
For a decently brought up horse to come
down to a hotel livery-stable is a trial I
never want to go through again. In the
field I never minded what came, but I do
hate musty corn and damp bedding.

"You girls would have laughed to see
the roan filly's face the first time we met
on the road.

"'Horse alive!' she cried, without so
much as a greeting, 'you don't mean to say
you have hopes? Why, Mr. Solitaire and
that horrid Mr. Lewis arrive to-day, and
the thing's probably as good as decided.'

" ' My Major is very resolute,' said I.

" ' So is a mule,' snapped Miss Gaiety, ' but we don't think the more of him for that.' "

The polo pony gave a horse laugh as he said, " *That* was one on you."

" It was," acknowledged Reveille; " and I regret to say it made me lose my temper to such an extent that I retorted, ' I can't say much for the taste of *your* woman ! '

" ' No,' assented the filly; ' if what you and Mr. Solitaire say is true, she 's taking the worse of the two. But then, a human can't help it. If you covered a horse all over with clothes, do you think any one would know much about him ? Moreover, two-thirds of what men do or say is said or done only to fool a woman. How can a girl help making mistakes, when she 's got nothing to go by but talk ? Why, look at it. Your Major seems balky most of the time, won't talk half of it, and when he does, says the things he should n't; while Mr. Lewis is always affable, talks well, and pays indirect compliments better than any man I ever met.'

" ' If she could only be told!' I groaned.

" ' She would be, if I could talk,' sighed the mare. ' I 'd let her know how he treats his horses!'

" ' Miss Gaiety,' I ejaculated, ' I 've got an idea.'

" ' What?' she demanded.

" ' Wait a bit till I 've had time to think it out,' said I. ' Gettysburg was n't fought in five minutes.'

" ' Gettysburg was a big thing,' she answered.

" ' So 's my idea,' I told her.

" In the meantime my Major was explaining to Miss Fairley that the government had sent him to New London to inspect the ordnance at Forts Trumbull and Griswold, and that he found it pleasanter to stay in Norwich, and run down by train to New London for his work. That 's the way humans lie when it does n't deceive any one and it is n't expected that it will. Of course Miss Fairley knew what brought him North, and why he preferred Norwich to New London! One thing he did do, though, which was pretty good. He apologised to her for having said what he did before their first ride, told her that his wound had been troubling him so that at times he scarcely knew what he was saying, and declared he'd been sorry ever since. He was humble! The Eleventh Battery of Light Artillery would never have known him.

"'There,' sniffed Miss Gaiety; 'if the idiot had only talked in that vein ten days ago, he might have done something. Oh, you men, you men!'

"At least he won a small favour; for when he asked leave, at parting, to be her companion the next day in a ride, she told him he might join her and Mr. Lewis, if he wished. But the permission was n't given with the best of grace, and she did n't ask him to luncheon before the start.

" I thought out my idea over night, and put it in shape to tell. My Major took me to the Fairleys' a little early, and so went

in, leaving me alone. In a minute, however, a groom brought the filly and the
grey round to the door, and with them
came Sagitta, the Russian wolf-hound,
whom, it seems, Mr. Lewis had brought
from Europe, and had just presented to
Miss Fairley.

"After the barest greetings, I unfolded
my scheme. 'I don't know,' said I, 'what
Mr. Sagitta thinks, but we three are a
spike-team in agreeing that Mr. Lewis
is a brute.'

"'I bow-wow to that,' assented the dog.
'He kicked me twice, coming up yesterday, because I was afraid to go up the
steps of the baggage-car.'

"'So far as we can see he is going to
win Miss Fairley,' I continued. 'As Miss
Gaiety says she's a dear, I think we ought
to prevent it.'

"'Very pretty,' says the grey; 'but, may
I ask, who is to interfere and put the hob-
bles on him?'

"'We are to tell her he's cruel.'

"'She won't understand us, if we tell

her till doomsday. These humans are so stupid!' growled Sagitta.

"'That's where my idea comes in,' I bragged — a little airily, it is to be feared. 'We can't, of course, tell it to her in words, but we can act it.'

"'Eh?' exclaimed the filly, with a sudden look of intelligence.

"'Not possible,' snorted the big grey.

"'I see,' cried the mare, her woman's wits grasping the whole thing in a flash, and in her delight she kicked up her hind legs in the most graceful manner.

"'Heyday!' exclaimed the grey, using our favourite expletive.

"It did n't take me long to explain to him and Sagitta, and they entered into the scheme eagerly. We were so hot to begin on it that we pawed the road all into holes in our impatience.

"Presently out came the three, and then the fun began. Mr. Lewis stepped forward to mount Felicia, and at once Miss Gaiety backed away, snorting. Then the groom left us, and tried to hold her.; but not a bit of it; every time Mr. Lewis tried to approach she 'd get wild.

"Finally my Major joined in by walking over to help, and the mare at once put her head round and rubbed it against him, and stood as quiet as a mouse. So he says: ' I 've only my left arm, Miss Fairley, but I think we can manage it;' and the next moment she was in the saddle.

"Lewis was pretty angry-looking as he went toward his own horse; and when he, too, began to back and snort and shiver, he did n't look any better, you may be sure of that. You ought to have seen it! The brute caught him by the bridle, and then the grey kept backing away or dodging from him. Out on the lawn they went, cutting it up badly, then into Miss Fairley's pet bed of roses, then smashing into the shrubberies. I never saw better acting. Any one would have sworn the horse was half dead with fright.

"It did n't take very much of this to make Lewis lose all self control.

" ' You cursed mule !' he raved, his face

white with passion; 'if I had a decent whip, I'd cut the heart out of you!' And suiting the action to the thought he struck the grey between the eyes with his crop a succession of violent blows, until, in his fury, he broke the stick. Then he clenched his fist and struck Solitaire on the nose, and would have done so a second time if Miss Fairley had n't spoken.

"'Stop!' she called hotly, and Lewis dropped his fist like a flash. Felicia was breathing very fast and her cheeks were white, while her hands trembled almost as much as Solitaire had. Her face wore a queer look as she continued: 'I — excuse me, Mr. Lewis, but I could n't bear to see you strike him. He — I don't think he — something has frightened him. Please give him just a moment.' Then she turned to my dear, saying, 'Perhaps you can calm him, Major Moran?'

"I should think he could! Talk of lambs! Well, that was Solitaire when my Major went up to him. He let himself be led out of the flower-bed back to the road as quiet as a kitten. The moment Lewis tried to come near him, however, back away he would, even from my confrère. The groom tried to help; but it takes more than three humans to control a horse who does n't want to be controlled.

"After repeated attempts they got tired of trying; and then Mr. Lewis suggested, with a laugh that did n't sound nice: 'Well, Major, we must n't cheat Miss Fairley of her afternoon; and since you seem able to manage my beast, perhaps you 'll ride him, and let me take yours?'

"Usually I should have been very much pained at my comrade's nodding his head, but this time it was exactly what I wanted. Whoop! Ride me? Neigh, neigh! If you ever saw a coward in an ague of a blue funk, that is what I was. I blessed my stars none of the Eleventh Battery were round! Lewis tried; but, do his best, I would n't let him back me. When my Major interfered, I sidled up to my dear just as if I could n't keep away from him; but when he attempted to hold me for

Lewis to mount, I went round in a circle,
always keeping him between me and the
brute.   It was oats to me, you'd better
believe, to see the puzzled, worried look
on Miss Fairley's face as she watched the
whole thing.

"Well, they discussed what they called
'the mystery,' and finally agreed that they
could n't ride that afternoon, so we horses
were sent down to the stable, and the three
went back to the verandah.   Sagitta told
me afterward what happened there.

"'Come here, pup,' calls Lewis to him,
the moment they were seated.

"Sagitta backed away two steps, bristling up, and growling a bit.

"'Come here, you brute!' ordered Lewis
hotly, rising.

"Sagitta crouched a little, drew his lips
away from his fangs, and pitched his growl
'way down in his throat.

"'Look out!   That dog means 'mischief,'
cried my Major.

"'Are the animals possessed?' roared
Lewis, his voice as angry as Sagitta's

snarl, yet stepping backwards, for it looked
as if the dog were about to spring.

"But my Major did n't retreat — not he!
He sprang between the wolf-hound and
Miss Fairley. 'Down, sir!' he ordered
sharply; and Sagitta dropped his lips and
his bristles, and came right up to him, wag-
ging his tail, and trying to lick his hand.

"'Is n't it extraordinary?' cried Miss
Fairley, with a crease in her forehead.
'Here, Sagitta!'

"'Miss Fairley, be careful!' pleaded my
Major; but there was n't the slightest necessity. Sagitta was by her side like a flash,
and was telling her how he loved her, in
every way that dog could. And there he
stayed till Lewis came forward, when he
backed away again, snarling.

"Now, in all their Washington inter-
course my Major had been the surly one;
but in the interval he had evidently had
time to realise his mistake, and to see that
he must correct it. Probably, too, he
was n't depressed by what had just taken
place. Anyway, that afternoon he was as

pleasant and jolly as he knew how to be. But Mr. Lewis! Well, I acknowledge he'd had enough to make any man mad, and that was what he was. Cross, sulky, blurting out disagreeable things in a disagreeable voice, with a disagreeable face: he did make an exhibition of himself, so Sagitta said.

"After as long a stay as was proper, my Major told them he must go, and I was brought round. Miss Fairley came to the stoop with him, and did n't I prick up my ears when I heard her say:

"'Since you were defrauded of your ride to-day, Major Moran, perhaps you will lunch here to-morrow, and afterward we will see if we can't be more successful?'

"The next day our interference was done a little differently. When we were brought round to the door, there was Mr. Lewis with a pair of cruelly big rowelled spurs on his boots, a brutal Mexican quirt in his hand, and a look on his face to match the two. Of course the grey gave him a lot of trouble in mounting, but we had already planned a different policy; and so, after enough snorting and trembling to make Felicia look thoughtful, he finally was allowed to get on Mr. Solitaire's back.

" Much good it did him! The filly and I paired off just as if we were having a bridle trip in double harness; but do his best, Mr. Lewis could not keep the grey abreast of us. Twenty feet in front, or thirty feet behind, that was where he was during the whole ride, and Lewis fought one long battle trying to make it otherwise. He had had the reins buckled to the lower bar of the curb, so it must have been pretty bad for the grey, but there was no flinching about him.

" Every now and then I could hear the blows of the quirt behind me; and when, occasionally, the grey passed us, I could see his sides gored and bleeding where they had been torn by the spurs, and bloody foam was all round his jaw, and flecked his chest and flanks. But he knew what he meant to do, and he did it without any heed to his own suffering. There was

joy when the filly told us that every time
the swish of the quirt was heard she could
feel her rider shiver a little; and Felicia
must have been distressed at the look of
the horse, for she cut the ride short by
suggesting a return home.

"Sagitta informed us afterward that if
Mr. Lewis had been bad the day before,
he was the devil that afternoon on the verandah, and Miss Fairley treated him like
one. What is more, she vetoed a ride for
the next day by saying that she thought
it was getting too cold to be pleasant.
When we had ridden away, Solitaire later
told me, she excused herself to Mr. Lewis,
and went to the stable and fed the grey with
sugar, patting him, and telling the groom
to put something on the spur-gashes.

"We horses did n't hear anything more
for three days, at the end of which time
my pal and I rode over one morning, and
reminded Miss Fairley that she had promised to show us where we should find some
fringed gentians; and though it was the
coldest day of the autumn, Felicia did n't

object, but ordered Miss Gaiety saddled, and away we went.

"We really had a very good time getting those gentians! Nothing was ever done with the flowers, however, owing to circumstances which constitute the most painful part of my confession. For a horse and an officer, I had been pretty tricky already, but that was nothing to the fraud I tried to perpetrate that morning. After our riders had mounted for the return to Yantic, I suggested to Miss Gaiety what I thought would be a winning race for my Major, which was neither more nor less than that she should run away, and let him save Miss Fairley. The roan came right into the scheme, and we arranged just how it was to be managed. She was to bolt, and I was to catch her; but since my Major had only his left arm, as soon as she felt his hand on the rein she was to quiet down; and I have no doubt but it would have been a pre-eminently successful coup if it had been run to the finish.

"What actually happened was that the mare bolted at a rabbit which very opportunely came across the road, and away she went like a shell from a mortar. I did n't even wait for orders, but sprang after her at a pace that would have settled it before many minutes. Just as I had got my gait, however, my poor dear gave a groan, reeled in his saddle, and before I could check myself he pitched from my back to the ground. I could not stop my momentum under thirty feet, but I was back at his side in a moment, sniffing at him, and turning him over with my nose, for his wounded arm was twisted under him, and his face was as white as paper. That was the worst moment of my life, for I thought I 'd killed him. I put my head up in the air, and did n't I whinny and neigh!

"The filly, finding that something wrong had happened, concluded to postpone the runaway, and came back to where I was standing. Miss Fairley was off her like a flash, and, kneeling beside my treasure, tried to do what she could for him, though that

really was n't anything.   Just then, by
good luck, along came a farmer in an ox-
cart.   They lifted my poor dear into it,
and a pretty gloomy procession took up
its walk for Yantic.

"When we arrived at the Fairleys' house,
there was a to-do, as you may imagine.
He was carried upstairs, while I went for
the doctor, taking a groom with me, because humans are so stupid that they only
understand each other. I taught that
groom a thing or two about what a horse
can do in the way of speed that I don't
believe he has ever forgotten."

"Did you do better than $1.35\frac{1}{2}$?" inquired the Kentuckian; but Reveille paid
no heed to the question.

"After that sprint I had about the
dullest month of my life, standing doing
nothing in the Fairleys' stable, while nearly
dying of anxiety and regret. The only
thing of the slightest interest in all that
time occurred the day after our attempted
runaway, when Mr. Lewis came down to
the stable, and gave orders about having

the big grey sent after him. He was n't a bit in a sweet temper — that I could see; and though I overheard one of the grooms say that he was to come back later, as soon as the nurse and doctors were out of the house, the big grey thought otherwise, and predicted that we should never see each other again. Our parting was truly touching, and put tears in the filly's eyes.

"' Friends,' said Solitaire, ' I don't think he will ever forgive me, and I suppose I am in for a lot of brutality from him; but I am not sorry. If you ever give me another thought please say to yourself: " He did his best to save a woman from having her life made one long night-mare by a cruel master."' .

" Nothing much happened in the weeks my Major was housed, with the exception of one development that had for me an extremely informing and delightful quality. One day, about a month after our cropper, Felicia came down to the stable, and without so much as a look or a word for Miss Gaiety, came straight into my stall, flung her arms about my neck, and laid her soft cheek caressingly against it, for some moments. Then she kissed me on the nose very tenderly, and offered me what I thought were some little white stones. I had never tasted sugar before, and nothing but her repeated tempting and urging persuaded me to keep the lumps in my mouth long enough to get the taste on my tongue. (I have to confess that since then I have developed a strong liking for all forms of sweetmeats.) What is more, she came down every day after that, and sometimes twice a day, to caress and feed me. There was no doubt about it, that for some reason she had become extraordinarily fond of me!

"It is awfully hard in this world to know what will turn out the best thing. As a matter of fact, the tumble off my back was about the luckiest accident that ever befell my Major; for it broke open the old wound, and as the local doctors did not have six hundred other injured men under them, they could give it proper attention, which the hospital surgeons had never been able to do. One of them extracted all the pieces of bone, set the arm, and then put it in a plaster jacket, which ought to have healed it in good shape very quickly. But for some reason it did n't. In fact, I became very much alarmed over the length of my Major's convalescence, till one day I overheard one of the stablemen say :

" ' Lor' ! He won't get well no too fast, with Miss Felicia to fluff his pillers, an' run his erran's, an' play to him, an' read aloud to him, an' him got nothin' to do but just lay back easy an' look at her.'

" Then I realised that it would be some time before he would feel strong enough to go back to his ordnance inspecting.

" Finally, one afternoon, the filly and I were saddled and brought round to the front door, and there were Miss Fairley and my Major, both looking as well and happy as their best friend would want to see them. It was a nice day, and away we went over the New England hills.

" There was n't much surliness or cool-
ness on that ride, and what they did n't
talk about is hardly worth mentioning.
After they had fairly cantered, conversa-
tionally, for over three hours, however, they
slowed down, and finally only Felicia tried
to talk, and she did it so jerkily and con-
fusedly, with such a deal of stumbling and
stammering, that presently, try her best,
she had to come to a halt, too. Then there
was a most awkward silence, until suddenly my Major burst out, more as if the
sentence were shot from a gun than as if
he were speaking it :

" ' Oh, Felicia, if you could only — '

" That seemed to me too indefinite a
wish to answer easily, and apparently Miss
Fairley thought the same, for another silence ensued which was embarrassing even
to me. So far as I could make out, my
Major could not speak, and Miss Fairley
would not. I was as anxious as he was to
know what she would say, and in my suspense I suddenly conceived an idea that
was little short of inspiration, though I

say it who ought not. I asked the roan filly:

"'Is your Felicia resting her weight on the side toward my Major, or on the side away from him?'

"'She has a very bad seat in her saddle,' the mare told me, 'and she is resting all her weight on the side next you.'

"'Then, Miss Gaiety,' I suggested, 'I think they will like it if we snuggle.'

"'Well, just for this once I will,' replied the filly, shyly."

Reveille turned in his stall, and, walking over to his manger, picked up a wisp of hay. But the action was greeted by an outburst from the ladies.

"Oh, you are not going to stop there, dear Mr. Reveille!" they chorused.

"I always did hate a quitter on the home stretch," chimed in the discontented cob, pleased to have a grievance.

The narrator shook his head.

"No gentleman," he asserted, "who overheard what followed would ever tell of it;

and a horse has an even higher standard of honour."

" Ah, darling Mr. Reveille," pleaded the feminine part of his audience, " just a little more ! "

" I hate to seem mulish," responded the horse, " and so I will add one small incident that is too good not to be repeated. When we rode up to the house that evening, shamefully late for dinner, my Major lifted Miss Fairley off Miss Gaiety in a way that suggested that she might be very breakable, and, after something I don't choose to tell you about, he said :

" ' I wonder if we shall ever have another such ride ! '

" ' It does n't seem possible, Stanley,' whispered my Felicia, very softly. ' You know, even the horses seemed to understand ! ' "

Just as Reveille finished thus, a human voice was heard, saying :

" You will have the veterinary see the cob at once, and let me know if it is a case which requires more than blistering."

Then came a second and very treble voice. " Papa," it begged, " will oo lif' me up on ol' Weveille's back ? " And the next moment a child of three was sitting astride the old warrior and clinging to his mane.

" Well, you old scoundrel," said the human, " do you know you are getting outrageously fat ? "

" Weveille is n't not any scoundwel," denied the child, earnestly. " Mama says Weveille is a' ol' darlin'. "

" Your mama, fortunately for Reveille and me, always had a soft spot for idiots," explained the man, stroking the horse's nose affectionately. " But I will say this for the old fellow : if most folly resulted as well as his, there would be a big premium on fools."

Reveille winked his off eye at the other steeds.

" Are n't these humans comical ? " he laughed.

A WARNING TO LOVERS

BEFORE some blazing logs, which fill a deep fireplace with warmth that overflows to just the right extent into the room, stands, slightly skewed, a sofa. The sofa is a comfortable one. It is short, deep, and low; and the arms have a suggestion of longing to be filled that is truly seductive. In addition, two down cushions imply that the sofa is quite prepared to fit itself to any figure, be it long, short, broad, or narrow. Altogether, it is a most satisfactory sofa.

But the satisfactoriness does not end here. Seated at one end of that sofa is a girl, clearly in that neither grass nor hay period, which begins at sixteen and ends at eighteen. Not that it is intended to suggest that because the girl is neither hay nor grass she is unattractive. Quite the reverse.   New-mown hay is the sweetest, and the girl, if neither child nor woman, is, in her way, just as sweet.

In algebra, when a, b, and c are computed, it is possible to find the unknown quantity x.   Applying an algebraic formula to the above, we at once deduce what is necessary to complete the factors. It may be stated thus : a, a sofa, plus b, a charming girl; and as a, a sofa, must be divided by two, we find the unknown quantity to be x, a man, and the product of our a, b, and x to equal xxx, or triple bliss.   Nor is this wrong.   The sofa does not do more than seat two people comfortably, yet at the present moment there are little spaces at both ends.   Concerning the other details of this $a \div 2 + b + x - o$ ($i.\ e.$ Mrs. Grundy), it seems needless to enlarge.

"And isn't it wonderful, Freddy, that you should love me and I should love you?" cooed the girl.

"Just out of sight," replied Freddy.

Most people would agree with the above

remarks, though the circumstance of a man and woman occasionally loving each other is a phenomenon recognised, if not approved, by science. But though these two did not know it, there was a wonder here. Freddy has been spoken of in the masculine gender, because, as Shakespeare wrote: "The Lord made him, therefore let him pass for a man." Otherwise his manliness was open to debate. Lovable the girl unquestionably was, or at least very fast verging upon it, but it passeth human intelligence how Freddy could inspire any sort of feeling except an intense longing for a gun loaded with goose-shot.

"And that we should have loved each other for so long, and never either of us dreamed that we cared one little bit for each other," continued the girl.

Freddy did not assent to this sentiment as readily as to the former. Freddy had been quite sure that Frances had been pining for his love in secret for some months. So he only remarked: "We got there all the same."

"Yes," assented Frances. "And we'll love each other always, now."

"But I say," inquired Freddy, "what do you think your father and mother will say?"

"Why, they'll be delighted," cried the girl. "It couldn't be better. Cousins, — and just the same age — and, and — Oh, lots of other reasons, I'm sure, but I can't think of them now."

"Let's tell them together," suggested Freddy, courageously.

"Freddy! Of course not. That isn't the right way. No, you must request an interview with papa in his library, and plead eloquently with him."

"I suppose I must," answered Freddy, with a noticeable limpness in his voice and vertebræ.

"Wouldn't it be fun if he should refuse his consent!" exclaimed the girl.

Freddy did not recognise the comical quality. "I don't see it," he moaned.

"Why, it would be so romantic! He would of course order you to leave the house, and never, never darken his doors again. That's what the father always does."

" You think that's fun ? "

"Such fun ! Then, of course, we should have to arrange for romantic meetings, and secret interviews, and you would write little letters and put them in a prayer-book in our pew; and watch to get a glimpse of me as I go in and out of places; and stand on the opposite side of the street each night, till you saw the light in my room put out. Oh! What fun it will be ! "

" It might be raining," complained Freddy.

" All the better. That would prove your devotion. Don't you love me enough to do that ? "

" Yes," said Freddy, meekly, " but I hate getting wet. Sometimes one catches a nasty cold."

" Any one who tells a girl he loves her with a fervour and passion never yet equalled by man should not think of such things," asserted Frances, disapprovingly.

Freddy had an idea that a girl who reciprocated such a passion should not seem so happy over the prospect of her lover undergoing the exposure, but the youth did not know how to express it. So he proposed: " Let's keep it a secret for the present."

" Let's," assented Frances. " We won't tell any one for a long time, but just have it all to ourselves. And when I am riding in the morning you must join me; the groom will think it's all right. And whenever papa and mama are to be out in the evening, I'll put a lamp in my window, and — "

Ting!

It seemed as if some of the electric current which made that distant muffled ring had switched and passed through the happy pair. Both started guiltily, and then both listened with the greatest intentness; so intensely, that after a moment's pause they could hear the soft gliding sound of the footman's list slippers as they travelled down the hallway;

could hear the click of the lock as he opened the front door; could hear the murmur of voices; could hear the door closed. Then, after a moment's silence, a voice, for the first time articulate to them, said : " I 'll wait in the morning-room."

" Freddy," gasped the girl, " it 's that horrid Mr. Potter.   Quick ! "

Both had arisen from the sofa, and Freddy looked about in a very badly perplexed condition.   He was quite willing, but about what was he to be quick?

" Sit down in that chair," whispered the girl, pointing to one at a more than proper distance, and Freddy sprinted for it, and sat down.   The girl resumed her seat on the little sofa, and putting her hands in a demure position, rather contradictory to her quick breathing and flushed cheeks, began : " As you were saying, the De Reszke brothers were the only redeeming — Oh ! Good evening, Mr. Potter."

" Good evening, Frances," responded a tall, rather slender, strong-featured man, attired in evening dress, who had leisurely strolled into the room, and who did not offer to go through the form of shaking hands. "Talking to the fire?"

"No. Freddy and I were chatting about the opera."

Mr. Potter put on his glasses and languidly surveyed the region of the fireplace. Then he turned and extended his investigation, till his eyes settled on Freddy, stuck away in the dim distance.

"Oh, are you there, youngster?" he remarked, in a tone of voice implying that the question carried no interest with it. He looked at his watch. "Isn't it rather late for you two?"

"It's only quarter past ten," answered Frances, bristling indignantly. "And if it were twelve it wouldn't make any difference." To herself she said, "How I hate that man! Just because he's thirty-four, he always treats us as if we were children; and the way he tramples on poor, dear Freddy is outrageous!"

"You don't seem to be very sociably

inclined," said Mr. Potter. "From the distance between you I should think you two chicks had been quarrelling. Come, make it up."

"Not at all," cried Frances, indignantly. "I never lose my temper; except when you are here."

"Is that the reason you have n't asked me to sit down?" asked Potter, smiling.

"Of course you are to sit down, if you want," exclaimed Frances. "Here." And she moved the four inches towards her end of the sofa that had not been occupied under the previous arrangement.

Mr. Potter seated himself leisurely in Freddy's old place, and arranged one of the cushions to fit the small of his back. "I came to say good-bye to your mother," he explained, "and as I'm too busy to stop in to-morrow, I decided to wait. You youngsters need n't think it necessary to sit up to entertain me. Won't Freddy's mother be sending his nurse for him if he stays much later?"

"I'm so glad you are going to Europe,"

remarked Frances. " I hope you 'll stay a long while."

Mr. Potter put his glasses on again and looked at Frances calmly. " Hello!" he said mentally, " the kitten 's learning how to hiss." Aloud he announced : " I shall only be gone for a month or two, — just the voyage and a change."

"What a pity!" responded Frances, bitingly.

" I thought you 'd miss me," replied Mr. Potter, genially.

Frances gave an uneasy movement on the sofa, a cross between an angry shake of the shoulders and a bounce.

" Where are you going?" questioned Freddy at this point, feeling that as a grown man he must bear his part of the chat.

" Look here, littleun," said Mr. Potter, "if you expect me to talk to you back there, you — " At this point he suddenly ceased speaking, as if something more interesting than his unfinished remark had occurred to him.

"Freddy found it too warm by the fire," explained Frances hastily, guilty at heart, if to outward appearance brazen. But Mr. Potter did not hear what she said, and sat looking into the fire with a suddenly serious look, which nevertheless had a laugh not very far underneath.

After quite a pause, Frances said: "How entertaining you are!"

"Yes," assented Mr. Potter, coming back from his thoughts; "I always enjoy myself, and I find that other people do the same." Then he again relapsed into meditation.

"Is n't he just as horrid as can be?" raged Frances, inwardly. "He believes just because some women think him clever, and because men like him, and because he's a good business man, and because mama's always praising him to his face, as she would any one who was papa's partner, that he is perfect. And no matter how you try to snub him, he is so conceited that he won't see it. Horrid old thing!" Aloud she asked, "What are you thinking about?"

Mr. Potter laughed. " That 's a great secret," he asserted.

* *
* *

An hour later, Mr. Potter was seated in a library, smoking, with a glass of seltzer — and something else — at his elbow. Opposite to him sat a man of perhaps twice his years, equally equipped with a cigar and seltzer — and something else.

" Well," remarked the senior, " I think if we can get the whole issue at 82½ and place them at 87 and accrued interest, we had better do it.'

" That 's settled then," agreed Mr. Potter. " Now, is there anything else? I don't want to have cablegrams following me, since I 'm going for a rest."

" No," replied the other. " I know I shall want my partner's advice often enough, but I 'll get on without you. Take a rest. You can afford it. There 's nothing else."

" Then if you are through with business, I want to speak to you of Frances," said Mr. Potter.

Mr. De Witt turned and looked at Mr. Potter quickly. "What about?"

"Do you know that that girl's grown up, and we none of us have realised it?"

"Well?"

"And do you know that she has seen next to no people, — that her morning ride, her studies, and her afternoon drive with her mother are the only events of her day?"

"Well?"

"And that her summers, off in that solitary country house of yours, with never a bit of company but Freddy De Witt and myself, are horribly dull and monotonous?"

"Well?"

"And that to kill time she reads a great many more novels than is good for any one?"

"Come, come, Champney, what are you driving at?"

"One more question. Mrs. De Witt and you are dining out almost nightly. What do you suppose Frances does evenings?"

"Does? Plays a bit, and reads a bit, and goes to bed like a good child."

"But I tell you she isn't a child any longer, so you can't expect her to behave like one. It dawned upon me this evening, and the quicker it dawns upon you the better."

"Why?"

"Do you want her to make a fool of herself over Freddy?"

"Freddy!"

"Yes, Freddy."

"Ridiculous! Impossible!"

"Because they are a long way towards it, and if you want to end it, you'll have to use drastic measures."

"Her own cousin, and only eighteen! I never heard of such folly."

"But I tell you those two think they are in love with each other, and if you don't do something, they'll really become so before long. Thinking a thing is two-thirds of the way to doing it, as is shown by the mind cure."

"I'll put an end to it at once," growled Mr. De Witt. "Never heard of such nonsense."

" And how will you end it? " inquired Mr. Potter, smiling a little.

" End it?   Tell them to stop their foolishness.   Send him about his business."

" I thought that would probably be your way.   Don't you think it would be better to get an injunction from the courts? "

" What good would an injunction do? " asked Mr. De Witt, crossly.

" Just as much good as your method. You can no more stop boys' and girls' love by calling it foolishness than the courts can.   If you do as you propose, you'll probably have a run-away match, or some other awful bit of folly."

" Well, what can I do? "

" The best thing is to pack your trunks and travel a bit.   That will give her something else to think about, and she'll forget all about the little chap."

" But I can't leave the business."

" The business will run itself.   Or, if it won't, what's a year's profits compared to your only daughter's life happiness? "

" But the bonds? "

" Don't bid on them."

" I can't go. I can't leave my business. Why, I have n't been away from it for more than a week in forty years."

" All the more reason for going now."

" I have it. Her mother and she shall sail with you."

" Oh, get out !" ejaculated Champney, " I 'm going for a rest." Mr. Potter had been the slave for many years of two selfish sisters and a whining mother, — a mother who loved to whine, — and womankind meant to him an absolute and entire nuisance.

" That 's it," said the senior partner, regardless of this protest. " You arrange to stay for six months instead of two. I 'll do your work gladly."

" I can't," groaned Potter.

" Come, Champney," wheedled the elder, " you say yourself that my little girl's life happiness depends on her going. For my sake ! Come ! I did a good turn for you — or at least you 've always said I did — in the partnership. Now do one for me."

Potter sighed. He was used to being martyrised where women were concerned and had not learned how to resist. "Well, if you say so. But I'll have to leave them there. Two months is my limit."

"All right," assented the senior, gleefully.

"Perhaps," thought Potter, "perhaps they won't be able to pack in time." And the idea seemed to please him.

For half an hour longer they chatted, and then Potter rose.

"Tell me, Champney," inquired the senior, "how did you find out about it?"

"Oh," laughed Champney, "that's telling."

* * *

The next day there was woe in Israel. Mr. De Witt was cross over the "children's folly," as he called it. Mrs. De Witt was deeply insulted at such sudden and peremptory marching orders. "Men are so thoughtless," she groaned; "as if one could be ready to go on a day's notice!"

Champney was blue over the spoiling of his trip. Freddy, when he heard the news, was the picture of helplessness and misery, and only added to the friction by coming round and getting in everybody's way, in the rush of the packing. As for Frances, she dropped many a secret tear into the trunks as her belongings were bestowed therein. Never, it seemed to her, had true love been so crossed.

"I know Mr. Potter is at the bottom of it." (Frances was not alluding to the trunk before which she knelt.) "He's always doing mean things, yet he never will acknowledge them. He won't even pay me the respect of denying them." Frances slapped a shawl she was packing, viciously. "To think of having to travel with him! He won't even look at me. No. He doesn't even pay me the compliment of looking at me. I don't believe he's even noticed my eyes and eyelashes." Frances gazed into a hand-glass she was about to place in the trunk, and seemed less cross for a moment after the scrutiny.

" He's just as snubby as he can be.   I
hate snubby people, and I'll be just as
snubby to him as I know how.   I'll — "

" Good afternoon, Frances," interrupted
a voice, which made that young lady nearly
jump into the trunk she was bending over.
" I came up to see if I could do anything
for you or your mother, and she sent me
in to ask you."

Frances was rather flushed, but that
may have been due to the stooping position.   " I don't think of anything," she
answered.

" I've had some chairs sent on board,
and laid in novels and smoked glasses and
puzzles ; and oysters, and game, and fruit,
and butter," said Champney, with a suggestion of weariness, " and I don't think of
anything else.   If you can suggest something more, I'll get it."

" I don't   know — Yes.   You might
change your mind and let us stay at
home," snapped Frances.

" Don't blame me for that," laughed
Champney."   That's your father's doings."

" I know you were at the bottom of it," charged Frances.

" My dear child —" began Champney.

" I 'm not *your* child, and I 'm not *a* child, and I won't be deared by you," cried Frances.

" Madame Antiquity," responded Champney, bowing, " I assure you, that far from wishing to force you to go on this trip with me, I only agreed to take you, at your father's request, and at a great personal sacrifice to myself."

Frances turned, and banged down the lid of her trunk. Then she banged it again, to get the hasp to fit. Then she picked up a pair of discarded boots and threw them across the room, hitting Freddy, who entered at that moment.

" Why, sweetness ! " gasped Freddy, who did not see Champney.

" Oh, go away," cried Frances, blushing. " Don't bother me ! Can't you see I 'm too busy to waste time now ? "

And to illustrate the callousness of man to true love, it is regrettable to state that

Champney slipped out of the door at this point, with an expression of great muscular tension about his mouth, and no sooner was he in the hall than the brute reeled up against the wall and, leaning there, laughed to a sinful degree.

Then he walked to the end of the hall, and entering a room, also cluttered with trunks, he sat upon one of them and re-told the scene to the woman packing. "I never saw anything so delicious in its way," he laughed. "I really believe the medicine's begun to work already. But do you know, Frances promises to be a tremendous beauty. Just now, when her cheeks and eyes were blazing so, she was simply glorious to look at." Which shows that Champney's cool, disregarding manner was not more than skin deep, and that unlimited possibilities lay underneath. Perhaps, too, another potion was beginning to work.

"I'm sorry she is so childish with you, Champney," said Mrs. De Witt.

"Don't trouble yourself about that. I really don't mind it; indeed, I am afraid I rather enjoy it. It's much rougher on her than on me, for she really feels it, and it's the person who loses his or her temper who suffers the most."

"I hope the dear child will try to be more amiable, for naturally she's sweetness itself, and it's bad enough to be saddled with us without making your trip worse than need be. It's so good of you to take us!"

"Dear lady," answered Champney, tenderly, "it's nothing but a little set-off against your years of goodness to me. You have really given me a second home; nothing I can ever do will make me other than your debtor."

"It's nice to hear you say so, Champney," said Mrs. De Witt, affectionately. "I have always felt as if you were a son of mine."

"Then don't talk to me about my goodness in taking you."

"But it is good of you."

"I don't think Freddy and Frances think so."

" Oh, Champney! Tell me, how did you find out their foolishness?"

" That is a secret," chuckled Champney, " that goes with me to the grave."

*
* *

Nor was it any better for Cupid the next day at the steamer. The evil genius of the little god, in the shape of Potter, persisted in following Frances about, and not a moment did she or Freddy find to swear constancy or anything else to each other. Only a hand squeeze, while the whistle was blowing " all ashore," did they get to feed their hearts upon during the separation.

Freddy went home, and, going to his room, flung himself on his bed, and moaned, and bit the pillow, and felt he was feeling great thoughts, and thought he was having great feelings.

And the little lady?

" No," she declared, " I don't want to walk with you; I don't want a steamer chair; I don't want anything; I only want to be left al-o-o-o-o-ne," and — running to her stateroom, she flung herself upon the lounge and wept over her unhappiness. "Oh, Freddy, Freddy," she sobbed, "only be true to me, that's all I ask."

But, alas, how is humanity constituted! The next morning, Freddy, after a final look at himself in a tall mirror, remarked to the vision: "Yes, that's very tony. Now, I'll take a walk on the Avenue, so as to give the girls a treat." As for Frances, after an hour's rapid walk with Champney in the crisp, sunny air, she came down to the breakfast-table, and said: "Yes, steward, I'll begin with fruit and oat-meal, and then I'll have chocolate, and beef-steak, and an omelette, and fried potatoes, and hot rolls, and marmalade. Oh! And, steward, do you have griddle cakes?"

Thus, despite their mutual intentions, the thought of each other lessened daily, till even the inevitable correspondence lost interest and flagged. Frances discovered that London, Paris, and the Riviera offered greater attractions than Freddy's witless and vapid "chronicle of small beer;" while Freddy found that listening to the conversation of a girl, present, was a far better way of spending time than reading the letters of a girl, absent. Finally, Frances found a letter at the bankers at Berne which ended the correspondence, — a letter over which she laughed so heartily that Champney looked up from his own bundle of mail and asked, "What is it that's so funny?"

"Freddy's engaged to Kitty Maxwell," replied Frances.

"I don't think you ought to be so gleeful at other people's misfortunes," reproved Champney, laughing himself, however, while speaking, as if he, too, saw something humourous in the announcement.

"I — I was n't — I was laughing at something else," Frances told him.

"What?" asked Champney.

"A secret," replied Frances, blushing a little, even while laughing.

"Not from me?" urged Champney.

"Yes; I sha'n't even tell you. Not a person in the world will ever know it, and I'm very glad," asserted Frances.

" I suspect I know it already," suggested Champney. " I am a great hand at finding out secrets. I have a patent method."

"What is that?" asked Frances.

" That, too, is a secret," laughed Champney.

*
* *

When next we meet any of our characters, they — or at least two of them — are toiling up a steep mountain path in the Bavarian Tyrol. Frances leads, for the way is narrow, and Champney follows. Conversation is at a marked discount; but whether this is due to the natural incompatibility of the two, or merely to the exertion of the climb, is unknown to history.

"She gets lovelier every day," finally remarked Champney.

Frances stopped, and turned. " What did you say?" she asked.

" I did n't speak," answered Champney.

" I 'm sure you did," said Frances.

" No," denied Champney, " I was merely thinking."

" You did say something, I 'm sure," responded Frances, turning, and resuming the climb.

Another five minutes brought them to the top of a little plateau set in between two ranges of mountains, and dividing two lakes, famous the world over. Even after the couple reached their destination, however, they stood silent for a minute. Then Frances exclaimed, —

" Is n't it glorious ? "

" Lovely," assented Champney, emphatically, but staring all the time at Frances, making it doubtful of what he was speaking.

Frances, being quite conscious of this gaze, looked all the harder at the view. " The mountains shut in so grandly ! " she remarked, after a pause.

" Such perfect solitude ! " said Champney, enthusiastically.

" Yes," assented Frances, with apparent reluctance in admitting the fact. " But I suppose we must be going down again ; mama will be lonely."

Champney calmly seated himself on a
stone, unstrung his field-glass, and surveyed through it the edge of the lake, far
below them.   "Your   mother," he announced, "is sitting on the rug, just where
we left her.   Her back is against the tree,
and she is pretending to read.   But she's
doing nothing of the kind.   She is taking
a nap on the sly.   Surely you don't want
to disturb her?"

"It must be nearly luncheon time."

"The boatmen have n't even begun to
unpack yet. Johann is just taking the
Vöslauer out of the boat, to cool it in
the lake.   They won't be ready for half
an hour."

Frances began to look a little worried.
There was a dangerous persistence in this
evident desire to remain on the alp.   "I
think I'll go down, anyway," she said.

"You must n't do that," begged Champney, laying the field-glass on the rock.

"Why not?" demanded Frances.

"Because I have something to say to
you," said Champney.

Silence and apparent interest in the view on the part of Frances.

"Do you know," asked Champney, "that I planned to be away for only two months?"

"Yes."

"And that I have been over here more than eight?"

"Oh, not so long as that," denied Frances.

"Eight months and four days."

"How quickly the time has gone!"

"But it has gone, and that's the trouble. I have decided that I *must* go back in September."

Frances hesitated, and then said bravely, "We shall be very sorry to have you go."

"That makes it all the harder," groaned Champney, rising and joining Frances. "In fact, I hate so to leave you" ("you" can be plural or singular) "over here that — that I want you to go back with me. Will you?"

"Why, that is for mama and papa to settle," remarked Frances, artfully dodging

the question, though perfectly understand-
ing it.

"This is n't to be settled by fathers
and mothers. My dar — my — I want
you to go — because you have become so
dear to me. I want to tell you — to tell
you how I have grown to love you in
these months. How happy you can make
me by a single word. I — you — once
you told me you were not 'my dear child.'
Oh, Frances, won't you be my dearest
love?"

"If you want me to be," acceded
Frances.

* * *

One of the simplest laws of natural
philosophy is that a thing descends more
easily than it ascends. Yet it took those
two over four times longer to come down
than it had taken them to go up, — which
proves that love is superior to all the laws
of gravity; though it is not meant to
suggest by this that it has aught to
do with levity. From among a variety
of topics with which they beguiled this

slow descent the following sentences are selected:

" I can't believe it yet," marvelled Champney. "It doesn't seem as if our happiness could have depended on such a small chance."

" What chance ? "

" Why — on that evening. When I found your mother wasn't in, I half turned away, but after hesitating, decided to wait. And then, when I found you two in the morning-room, I decided that I would leave you, and go and read in the library. I was just about to say so, when you told me to sit down by you on the sofa. That led to our coming off here together, and really finding out about each other. Of course that was equivalent to my falling desperately in love."

" But you could have done that at home," laughed Frances, merrily.

" No, I should have come off here, and some other man would have won you."

"Champney! I never could love any one but you."

Champney swallowed the absurd state-
ment rapturously. " That 's just like the
angel that you are," he declared.

" But I knew you had something to
do with our coming," asserted Frances,
" though you did deny it."

" No ; like a consummate donkey, I
did n't want to be bothered with you.
Conceive of it, dear one, that I could
ever think you a bother ! "

" You did n't know me," laughed
Frances happily, and with no intention
of vanity.

" No, I should think not. I wanted
your father to take you. But I shall never
want any one else to do that in the future."

" But why did you want me to go to
Europe, if it was n't to be with me ? "

" Why — um — because, dear one, I
saw a little girl that night who was longing so for love that she was accepting a
cheap and flashy counterfeit in its stead.
I did n't want her to waste a real heart on
such an apology for a man, and so I
interfered."

"But how did you know?" cried Frances, looking bewildered. "We had only just — you could n't have known it then?"

"Yes."

"How?"

Champney laughed as he replied: "That 's telling."

*
* *

And now, another leap, please, back to that fireplace, and sofa, again occupied by two — but not the same two — or, at least, only half the same.

"Well," groaned Champney, "I suppose I ought to be going, for you must look your prettiest to-morrow, otherwise malicious people will say it 's a match arranged for the business."

"Let them," laughed Frances. "By the way, how have you arranged about that? You are such a good business man, and papa and mama are so delighted, that I know you have the best of it."

"Of course I have. And she 's sitting beside me now. But nothing mercenary

6

to-night, Madam," ordered Champney. "Cupid, not cupidity."

" Well, Champney, dear, at least do tell me how you found out about — about — " Frances stopped there.

" Never." persisted Champney, nestling back on the sofa and laughing.

" I don't think it's nice for a man to have secrets from his wife," reproved Frances, taking an eminently feminine view of man's knowledge.

" That is to be," corrected Champney.

" Will you tell me — after to-morrow ? "

" No."

" Why not ? "

" It's too good to be told."

" Ah, Champney ! " And a small hand strayed round his neck, and rested lightly against his cheek. Champney looked very contented.

" Please, dear." And a pair of lips came dangerously close to his own.

Champney groaned a satisfied groan. " Well," he began, " do you remember when I came in the evening before we sailed, how Freddy was sitting over there, and you were sitting just where you are?"

"Yes."

"And how you let me sit down here, just where I am?"

"Yes."

"And how I chatted for a moment and then suddenly became silent?"

"Yes."

"That was when I discovered it."

"How?"

"I found that the seat I was sitting in was *warm!*"

"SAUCE FOR THE GOOSE IS SAUCE FOR THE GANDER."

"SAUCE FOR THE GOOSE IS SAUCE FOR THE GANDER"

֍

"OH, my dear!" cried her mother. "I hope you have properly considered? He is charming, of course, but — well — he is such a club habitué."

"What? Well, well!" exclaimed her father. "Bless me, Meg, I had no idea — Give me a kiss, if you have any to spare for your old dad now. Why, of course, I consent, if you care for him. Only tell Mr. Tyler I hear he spends too much time at his clubs."

"Margaret! How nice!" ejaculated her sister. "I've liked him from the start, and hoped — people said he was too fond of his club ever to care to marry, and so I thought — but now it's all right."

"I knew he meant biz," asserted her brother, "the moment he began to keep away from the club, and put in so much time with you."

"I cannot tell you, my dearest Margaret (if I may call you that?)," wrote his mother, "how happy I am over what my dear boy has just told me. The luxury and ease of club life are now so great that I had almost feared Harry could not be weaned from them. But since he has chosen such a dear, beautiful, and clever girl, my worst anxiety is over."

"You are indeed to be congratulated, niece," declared her aunt. "He is a most eligible *parti* — good looks, position, and wealth. If you can only keep him away from his clubs, I am confident you will be a very happy and domestic couple."

"I have been certain of it for weeks," her dearest feminine friend assured her. "There is n't a man I would rather have had you take, for he is so much at his club that I shall still see something of you."

"Er, Miss Brewster," said one of her rejected lovers, "let me offer you my

best wishes.   At the club we all swear by
Harry, and we actually think of going into
mourning over the loss.   Er, the fellows
are laying bets as to whether we shall ever
see him there again.   The odds are six
to one on the club, — but the fellows don't
know you, you know."

" I want to offer you my heartiest con-
gratulations," gushed the girl who had
tried for him.   " Mr. Tyler has always been
one of my best friends, and I am sure you
will be very happy.   He isn't, of course,
very fond of women's society, but—   Have
you asked him to resign from his clubs ? "

*
* *

" Don't you want to sit down, Harry ? "
asked Margaret, making room on the little
sofa beside the fire.

The young couple had enjoyed four
months of ecstatic travel, thirty days of
chaos while they settled their household
gods, and then a recurring Indian-summer
honeymoon of two months in front of
their own fireside in the charmingly cosey
library where the above remark was made.

Upon this particular evening, however, Harry, in following his wife from the dining-room, took neither his customary seat beside his wife on the sofa nor lighted a cigar. On the contrary, he stood leaning against the mantel with anything but an expression or attitude of ease, and, noting this, Margaret had asked her question.

"Not to-night, dear," said Harry. "The truth is — well — I met Parmlee on my way up town, and I — that is — he asked me to come round to the club this evening — and, well — I didn't like to disappoint him. And then, a fellow must n't stag — that is — don't you think, my darling, that it's a mistake for married people to see too much of each other — and —"

"Oh, Harry!" cried Margaret, interrupting and rising. "You said you never could have enough —"

"And I can't, dearest," interrupted Harry, hurriedly. "But you know — Well — can't you —"

"I feel as if it were the beginning of the end," said Margaret, wildly.

"Now, my darling," pleaded Harry, "do be reasonable. You know — There, don't cry. I won't go. Sit down here and let me tell you how much I love you."

This occupied some time, but the clock never told on them, so it is impossible to say just how long. Presently Margaret said:

" Harry, did you really want to — to leave me ? "

" Not a bit," lied Harry. " It was only to keep my word to Parmlee."

" I suppose it 's too late now? " questioned Margaret, hopefully.

" Late? Oh, no! Fun's just beginning. But I 'm going to stay with you, sweetheart."

There was a moment's silence, and then Margaret said : " If you want to go, I want you to do it, Harry."

" Well," responded Harry, rising, " if you insist, dearest."

" I do," assented Margaret, in the most faint-hearted of voices.

" That 's a darling ! " said her husband.

" It 's half-past nine, so you 'll only have a few minutes of loneliness before you go to bed."

" I sha'n't go to bed, Harry," sighed Margaret, dolefully.

"Why, my darling," protested Harry, a little irritably, " you don't want to make me miserable thinking of you as here by yourself. Please be reasonable and don't sit up for me. Leave me free to come home when I want."

" Very well, Harry," acceded Margaret, dutifully, " if you insist I won't wait for your return."

Harry took the charming face in his hands, and kissed each eyelid, and then the lips. " I don't deserve such an angel," he asserted, his conscience pricking him, " and— Oh, hang Parmlee!" he growled, as her eyes, a little misty, looked up into his own. However, she belonged to him, and there were plenty of evenings, and — well — " Good-night, my trea-sure," he ended.

*
* *

Margaret remained standing where Harry had left her until she heard the front door close; then she collapsed on the sofa and softly sobbed her sense of desertion and grief into the pillow. The warnings of her family and friends recurred to her, and added to the pain of the moment a direful dread of the future. Not knowing that most bachelors are regular club men merely because it is the nearest approach to home life they can attain, she dwelt on his having been apparently wedded to these comforters of men, before marriage, and inferred a return to his former daily frequenting of them.

Her grief was keen enough to prevent her from noticing that the front door was presently opened, and not till she heard a faint cough in the room did she raise her head from the pillow. It was to find a servant with his back turned to the sofa, occupied, apparently, in setting a chair in a position entirely unsuited to it, — a proceeding he made far more noisy than became a well-trained butler, and which he accompanied with two more coughs.

Hurriedly wiping her eyes, Margaret asked, "What is it, Craig?"

With his eyes carefully focussed to see everything but his mistress's face, the man came forward and held out his tray.

Almost mechanically she took the card upon it, and after a mere glance she directed, — "Say that Mrs. Tyler is not receiving this evening, and begs to be excused."

Left alone once more, the young wife sat down upon a stool near the fire, and looked into the blaze, idly twirling the card. "I wonder," she soliloquised presently, "if he would have done the same." Again she lapsed into meditation, for a few minutes; then suddenly she sat up straight, with an air of sudden interest which was clearly derived from her own thoughts. A moment later, she gave a short, hesitating laugh. "If I only dared! I wonder if he would? Men are —" she said disconnectedly; but even as she spoke her face softened. "Poor dear!" she murmured tenderly. Yet the words of pity melted into another laugh, and this time merriment and not guilt was as the dominant note. Springing to her feet with vivacity, she sped into the hall, and placed the card on the tray, and that in turn conspicuously on the hatrack. A second action consisted in turning on all the electric lights of the chandelier. This done, she touched the bell.

"You may close the house, Craig," she ordered, when the servant responded to the summons, "but as Mr. Tyler has gone to his club, I wish you to leave these lights just as they are. I prefer that he should not come home to a darkened house, so don't turn out one." Giving one last glance, half merry and half guilty, at the bit of pasteboard put in so prominent a position, Margaret lightly tripped upstairs, humming something to herself.

* * *

Meantime Harry had wended his way to the club.

" Hello, Tyler ! " said the man his wife had refused. " Don't mean to say you 've actually ceased to be one of the ' submerged tenth ? ' How and where is your superior moiety ? "

" When I left Mrs. Tyler before her fire, ten minutes ago, she was very well."

" By George, if I had as clever and pretty a wife I don't think I should dare to leave her alone. I should be afraid of the other men."

Harry turned away to hide his frown, but as he went towards the door of the billiard room, rejoined : " Perhaps it would n't be safe with *your* wife." To himself he carolled gleefully : " That cuts both ways."

" But you are not afraid, I understand," called the man, irritatingly, " so I take it you won't mind if I drop round there for a few moments this evening, eh ? "

" Certainly not, " responded Harry, suavely, but gritting his teeth. " Hang the fellow," he muttered. " How do such cads ever get into decent clubs? As if Margaret's refusing him twice was n't enough to make him understand that she does n't want him round!"

Tyler's anger was quickly forgotten in the warm reception his cronies gave him, and a tumbler of "unsweetened" and a cue quickly made him forget both the incident and the passing hours. Not till the marker notified the players that the time limit had come did he wake to the fact that it was two o'clock.

With a sense of guilt the husband hurried home. In the hallway, as he took off hat and coat, he noticed the card, and picked it up. "So he did come," he growled, with a frown. "I hope Meg had gone to bed before he got here. Not, of course, that it really matters," he went on. "She told me she never could endure him, so he's welcome to call as often as he likes to be snubbed." To prove how little he cared, the husband crushed the card viciously, and tossed it on the floor.

The light in Margaret's room was burning low, Harry noticed when he had ascended the stairs, and, peeping in, he saw that she was sleeping peacefully. Entering quietly, he looked at her for a moment, thinking with a little pang that he had given her pain. "You don't deserve such an angel," he said aloud. "See how she has done just what you asked her to do, with never a word of — There is n't another woman who would have taken it so sweetly. You 're an ass! And for what? Four hours of — of nothing, when I might have been with her." He leaned down to very softly kiss a stray curl, and went towards his own room, while saying: "How pretty and dainty she is! She's worth all the clubs in the world!" What was more, for a minute he believed it.

The moment Harry was gone Margaret opened her eyes very wide, rose softly, and looked at the clock. Then she went back to bed, smiling demurely.

*
* *

The next morning, when Harry entered the breakfast room a little late, he was received with a kiss, and no word of reproach. Margaret chatted over the meal in her usual entertaining, happy mood, telling him the news she had already extracted from the morning's paper.

"She's too clever ever to nag a man," thought Harry, and assured that he was not to be taken to task, he became equally amiable, and told her whom he had seen at the club, and of his score.

"I'm glad you had such a pleasant evening!" said Margaret, sweetly. "I hope you didn't stay so late as to tire yourself."

"I didn't notice the time," fibbed Harry, "but probably I was in by twelve."

"Oh, no, dear," said Margaret, pleasantly, "for I didn't get home till after one myself, and you weren't back then."

* * *

Twenty times Harry has tried to persuade his wife into acknowledging that she spoke in jest, but Margaret only looks at him with wideopen, questioning eyes, as innocent as a child's. Her husband firmly believes that she went to bed ten minutes after he left the house, and always ends his unsuccessful attempts to get her to confess the fact by taking Margaret in his arms and telling her of his belief. This faith his wife rewards with a tender kiss, but only a kiss, and still maintains her demure silence.

Harry spends no more evenings at the club, and every woman who knows him holds him up to other men as an ideal married Benedick.

THE CORTELYOU FEUD

THE CORTELYOU FEUD

❦

IT could never have happened to us anywhere in New York but at Mrs. Baxter's. I say this not with bitterness at, but in calm recognition of, the merits and demerits of that universally esteemed lady. Abroad, with the lords chamberlain, herald's offices, and peerages, it would be impossible. In the far West, where the biography and genealogy of the leading families are not subjects for polite conversation, it might occur frequently. But in New York, lying between these two extremes, one is safe, except from accidents due to the unfortunate existence of a peculiar class of people.

The kind I refer to are those described as having a good heart. Such an organ involves, as a natural corollary, a weak head. These qualities in combination are a terrible menace to society; for, owing

to the very goodness of heart, their posses-
sors are pardoned over and over again, and
repeat their ill deeds with as much im-
munity from punishment as a New York
police captain. Every social circle has
one or more of these half-criminals, and in
that in which my lot was cast Mrs. Baxter
was unequalled for the number, ingenuity,
and innocence of her mistakes. Omitting
all hearsay and they-say knowledge, I was
her forty-seventh victim; and as pœnolo-
gists affirm that more than half of the
criminal acts are undiscovered, it can at
once be seen how society is menaced by
people with good hearts.

The lady who always tells me when I
do wrong — and to married men I need
not be more descriptive — has held me
responsible for that evening; and, since
she married me, her husband is not the
one to impeach her discrimination. She
insists that, knowing Mrs. Baxter, I should
have come early, and so had time to arrange matters quietly. I appeal to any
man if it would ever occur to him to get

to a dinner early on the possibility he was to sit next a lighted shell, in order that he might express to his hostess his dislike of explosives. All New York has known for years of our family feud. It's been common property ever since our esteemed ancestors thrashed it out in court, to the enjoyment of the public and the disruption of our family. For thirty years dinners, luncheons, yacht cruises, and house parties have been arranged so as to keep a proper distance between the descendants of my grandfather John Cortelyou and of his nephew Dabney. Sometimes I have seen one of the latter at the opposite end of a large dinner-table, and here and there I have had other glimpses of them. But until that evening, no matter how close chance brought us together, we had always succeeded in maintaining a dignified unconsciousness of each other's existence.

I was, let it be confessed, thirty minutes late, and merely accepting the last little envelope on the tray the footman offered me, hurried towards the drawing-room. On my way I naturally looked at the card inside and read:

Mr. Pellew.
Miss Cortelyou.

That meant nothing to me. The name is not an uncommon one, and I have taken in my aunts often enough to get accustomed to the occurrence, even in the family. So, without a second thought of the matter, I passed through the doorway and discharged my devoirs with Mrs. Baxter.

" I was on the point of suicide, thinking you had failed me," she said. " As it is, Mr. and Mrs. Dana have just sent me word that they can't come because Milly has croup."

"My note said half after seven," I stated boldly. When one is very late it is always best to put one's hostess in the wrong, and a mistake more or less to Mrs. Baxter was immaterial.

"Oh, never!" she declared, so guiltily

that I was really sorry for her. "Well, we can't discuss it now. We were just going in without you, and we'll go on, leaving you to find your partner by the process of elimination. I haven't left you Hobson's choice, however."

I glanced round, and as the couples had gravitated together, I easily picked out the only single figure left, and went towards it. She was turned from me, standing by Ferdie Gallaudet and his partner, who had not yet moved.

"That back is too young and pretty for Aunt Ellen or Madge," was my first thought. My second was a spoken one, and merely consisted of the trite, "I am to have the pleasure, Miss Cortelyou."

She was saying something to the girl, and went on saying it, with her head over her shoulder, even as she rested her hand on my arm and let me lead her away. And just as I was going to look at her, I caught sight of Ferdie's face, and fell to wondering what could ail him that he looked so queer. We had been close to the door, and before she had finished her remark, or I had ceased from wondering, we were through it and in the half-gloom of the hall.

"I beg your pardon," said she, turning to me, and speaking very sweetly. "It was a message, and I had only just begun when you came."

"What a nuisance messages are!" was my remark. "What a nice voice you have!" was my thought. Then we entered the dining-room, and I glanced at my partner. It was Kate Cortelyou!

She looked at me at the same moment, and as our eyes met, an expression of consternation appeared on both our faces. At least, that's what I felt in myself and saw in her. Horror succeeded as a next sensation and expression. Womanlike, she cast her eyes appealingly towards her hostess, and, manlike, I took a step towards the hall door. In another second I think I should have bolted, but just then Ferdie Gallaudet said, "Here's your seat, Jack," with a grin like a Cheshire cat

on his face. I looked at Kate and she
looked at me. Then we both looked at the
chairs. Mechanically I stepped to them
and pulled out that on the right of mine.
Kate's eyelashes fluttered for a moment,
as if she were hesitating; then she slipped
into the seat, and the next moment I
was sitting beside her. But enchant-
ingly pretty as I thought her (and I was
either too fair-minded or she was too
beautiful for me not to acknowledge it,
however much I might dislike to do so),
I could only wish I had broken my leg
on my way to the house.

I turned to my left to see if any escape
were possible, but my neighbour on that
side was that horrible perpetual motion
of a Mrs. Marvin, and, besides, she was
very properly occupied with her partner.
I peered furtively behind Kate to see if
she could escape me, for anything was
better than the alternative. Next her
were two empty seats. Mrs. Baxter's
capacity for social blundering had done
its worst.

There is this to be said for the Cortelyou women, whether friends or enemies: I've never seen one show the white feather in action. Just as I was preparing to collapse under this accumulation of horrors, Kate turned to me, with the friendliest of smiles, and murmured, —

" It's ghastly, but every one except Mrs. Baxter is watching us."

I took a furtive glimpse of the other guests. They were all pretending to talk, but all clearly were missing nothing of our *tableau vivant*. Was n't she clever to have seen it so quickly?

" They hope we 'll make a show of the family for their benefit," I growled.

" Can't we — " suggested Kate, and then hesitated, and blushed very prettily. The Cortelyou women are plucky, but Kate was only nineteen.

I never was good as leader, but at the shafts I 'm steady and reliable. " Of course we can," I responded, won by that blush.

" Don't frown, then," smiled Kate.

" I was not frowning at you," I protested

" But they 'll think you are," she replied.

I tried to appear as pleased as Kate so successfully pretended to be, and she rewarded me with an encouraging " That 's better," and a very refreshing look at her eyes.

" Now," she continued, " how can we do it ? "

" I 'm pretty well up on the litany," I whispered. " If you can do the supplications I can respond with the 'miserable sinner' part."

Kate laughed merrily, even while shaking her head reprovingly. Kate has nice teeth. " You are painfully frank," she told me.

" Frank ? "

" Yes. You are probably not a bit more miserable than I am, but I don't groan aloud."

" Oh, I say ! " I exclaimed, rather horrified at the construction my speech had been given. " It would be pure form, you know, quite as it is in church, and not mean a bit more than it does when the sinner 's pretty and wears a French gown."

Kate drew her mouth down into a church-going expression, which was very fetching in its demureness, but which was n't suitable for our public performance, so I remarked:

"Don't look so disapproving. The saintly vein suits the Madonna type, but the Cortelyou forte lies in quite another direction."

I won another laugh from those unsaintly lips. "You are worse than I thought," she added.

"Then you have thought of me?" I inquired, beginning to mellow under her laugh. That was a mistake, for her face instantly became serious, and her eyes gave a flash.

"What I think is my own concern," she responded. The Cortelyou women are stunning when they look haughty.

Being one of the family, however, I am too accustomed to the look to be as entirely crushed by it as others are. "Who's frowning now?" I asked. I thought I'd learn what kind of a temper Kate had.

She still smiled as if she liked being put next me, but her eyes gleamed, and I knew she'd pay me for my speech if the opportunity occurred.

"We can't begin like this," she said. "Suggest something else."

"I once heard of a poor couple in an English county who were always sitting next each other, so they agreed to count alternative tens up to a thousand," I answered.

"I'm afraid you have n't enough facial control for that," replied Kate, sweetly, appearing the picture of contentment. I thought her remark unnecessary, considering we had been face to face only a few minutes, and that she had just lost control of hers.

"Then suggest something yourself," I muttered.

"As the photographer says, 'A little more smile, please,'" corrected Kate. "Yes, you unquestionably have the Cortelyou temper," she added serenely.

"If I had," I asserted, "I should long since have turned to Mrs. Marvin, who is dying for a listener." I thought I'd let Kate understand *I* was n't sitting next two empty chairs.

She realised my advantage, but she would n't retreat. The Cortelyou women never do. Yet she knew enough to allow the honours of war to a hard-driven enemy. " The Cortelyou men are gentlemen," she said. Was n't that a neat way of telling me that I would never fail a woman in distress? I felt pleased that she understood the family so well as to have no fear for the conduct of even her bitterest enemy. " Besides," she continued, " I like the Cortelyou temper."

I raised my eyebrows.

" Yes," she persisted, " it 's an absolutely reliable factor. Now, papa — " Then she hesitated, realising the slip.

With an older girl I should have let her flounder, and enjoyed it; but she was so young, and blushed so charmingly that I had to help her out. " Don't keep me in suspense about your father," I said, in my most interested of tones, as if I truly

wished to know something of that blot on
the 'scutcheon.   This was my second mistake, and a bad one.

"We 'll leave Mr. Dabney Cortelyou
out of the conversation, please," she retorted, looking me in the eyes.   Was there
ever a meaner return for an act of pure
charity than that?

By the way, Kate's eyes are not Cortelyou.   I wondered from where she got them.
When we are angry we contract ours,
which is ugly.   She opens hers, which is
— I tried to make her do it again by saying, "You should set a better example,
then."   No good: she had got back to her
form, and was smiling sweetly.

"They are furiously disappointed so
far," she remarked.

"What an old curiosity shop the world
is about other people's affairs!   It's no
concern of theirs that my grandfather and
your" — I faltered, and went on — "that
my grandfather had a row in his family.
We don't talk of it."   When I said "we"
I meant the present company, but unfor-

tunately Kate took it to mean our faction,
and knowing of her father's idle blabbing,
she did n't like it.

"Your side has always dodged public-
ity," she affirmed viciously, though smiling winsomely.   Kate's smile must be her
strong card.

"We have maintained a dignified
silence," I responded calmly; but I knew
that a dagger thrust below that beautifully
modelled throat would be less cruel.

She tried to carry the wound bravely.
"My father is quite justified in letting the
truth be known," she insisted.

"Then why don't you, too, give public
house-warmings in the family-skeleton
closet?" I inquired blandly.   That was
really a triumph, for Kate had never talked
to outsiders about the wretched business.
She could n't even respond with what she
thought; for if she said that it was always
the side in the wrong which talked, she
was no better off, because we, like her,
had kept silence, but her father had chat-
tered it all over town.   She looked down,

and I gloated over her silence, till suddenly I thought I saw a suggestion of
moisture on her down-turned lashes.
What I said to myself was not flattering,
and moreover is not fit for publication.
What I said aloud I still glow over with
pride when it recurs to memory.

"Beware of the croquette!" I exclaimed
hastily. "I've just burned my tongue horribly." And I reached for the ice-water.

She was as quick as I had been. The
Cortelyou girls are quick, but she — well,
I think the ancestress who gave her those
eyes must have been a little quicker.

"You spoke a moment too late," she
replied, looking up at me. "I had just
done the same, and feel like weeping."
I wonder what the recording angel wrote
against those two speeches?

Then suddenly Kate began to laugh.

"What is it?" I queried.

"Taste your croquette," she suggested.

It was as cool as it should have been
hot!

We both laughed so heartily that Mr.

Baxter called, "Come; don't keep such a good story to yourselves."

"Pretend you are so engrossed that you did n't hear," advised Kate, simulating the utmost interest. "Are n't we doing well?"

"Thanks to you," was my gallant reply.

"Thanks to the Cortelyous," she declared.

"They might have known," said I, "that we'd never have a public circus to please them."

"Is n't it nice," she responded, "since we had to have a fracas, that it should be between ladies and gentlemen?"

"Is n't it?" I acceded. "Just supposing there had been some cad concerned, who would have written to the papers and talked to reporters!"

"That was impossible, because we are all Cortelyous," explained Kate. I like a girl who stands up for her stock.

"Yes," I assented. "And that's the one advantage of family rows."

"I want to tell you," she went on, "that you do my father a great injustice. Some natures are silent in grief or pain, and some must cry out. Because he talks, merely means that he suffers."

I longed to quote her remark about leaving her father out of the conversation, but having told her there were no cads in the family, the quotation was unavailable. So I merely observed, "Not knowing Mr. Dabney Cortelyou, I have had no chance to do him justice."

"But what you hear —" she began, with the proudest of looks; and it really hurt me to have to interrupt her by saying, —

"Since I only get word of him from his dearest friends I am forced to take a somewhat jaundiced view of him."

"I suppose you are surrounded by toadies who pretend to know him," she said contemptuously.

I was not to be made angry. I was enjoying the dinner too much. "It would be a very terrible thing for our mutual friends," I continued, " if the breach were ever healed, and we exchanged notes as to their tattling."

" Fortunately they are in no danger," she answered, more cheerfully — indeed I might say, more gleefully — than it seemed to me the occasion required.

" Fortunately," I agreed, out of self-respect. Then I weakened a little by adding, " But what a pity it is you and I did n't have the settling of that farm-line !"

" My father could not have acted otherwise," she challenged back.

" And the courts decided that my grandfather was right."

" I should have done just as he did," she replied.

" Then you acknowledge my grandfather was right ? "

" I ! " — indignantly.

" You just assured me you should have done as he did ! " I teased, laughing. " No. Of course both of them were justified in everything but in their making a legal matter a family quarrel. If we had had it to do, it would have been done amicably, I think."

" What makes you so sure ? " she asked.

" Because I am sweet-tempered, and you — "

She would n't accept a compliment from an enemy, so interrupted me with, " My father has one of the finest natures I have ever known."

" ' Physician, know thyself,' " I quoted, getting in the compliment in spite of her.

" That's more than you do," she replied merrily.

This could be taken in two ways, but I preferred to make it applicable to her rather than to myself. I said, " Our acquaintance has been short."

" But we know all about the stock," she corrected.

" I 'm proud of the family," I acknowledged ; " but don't let 's be Ibsenish."

" I knew you did n't like him," said Kate, confidentially. " I don't either."

" He 's rather rough on us old families," I intimated.

"Sour grapes," explained Kate. "The would n't-because-I-can't-be people always stir up the sediments of my Cortelyou temper."

"I thought you liked the family temper," I suggested.

"In anybody but myself," she told me. "With others it's really a great help. Now, with my brothers, I know just how far I can go safely, and it's easy to manage them."

"I suppose that accounts for the ease with which you manage me."

She laughed, and replied demurely, "I think we are both on our good behaviour."

"I'm afraid our respective and respected parents won't think so."

This made her look serious, and I wondered if her father could be brute enough ever to lose that awful temper of his at such a charming daughter. The thought almost made me lose mine. "They can't blame you," I assured her. "Your father —"

" Is sure that everything I do is right,"
she interjected, " but Mrs. Pellew? "

" We will not make Mrs. Pellew — "

Kate saw I was going to use her own
speech, and she interrupted in turn. " Of
course you are over twenty-one," she
continued, " but the Cortelyou women
always have their way. I hope she won't
be very bad to you."

She certainly had paid me off, and to
boot, for my earlier speech. And the
nasty thing about it was that any attempt to answer her would look as if I
felt there was truth in her speech, which
was really ridiculous. Though I live with
my mother, my friends know who is the
real master of the house.

" Any one living with a Cortelyou woman must confess her superiority," I responded, bowing deferentially.

" Yes," she said, nodding her head know-
ingly. " People say that she spoils you.
Now I see how you compass it."

" We have only exchanged Ibsen for
Mrs. Grundy," I complained.

"'Excelsior' is a good rule," announced Kate.

"That's what you'll be doing in a moment," said I, trying to look doleful, for we were eating the game course.

"How well you act it!" replied Kate. "You ought to go on the stage. What a pity that you should waste your time on clubs and afternoon teas!"

"Look here," I protested, "I've done my best all through dinner, considering my Cortelyou temper, and now, just because it's so nearly over that you don't need me any longer is no reason for making such speeches. I don't go to my club once a week, and I despise afternoon teas."

"That sampler has become positively threadbare," retorted Kate. "I really think it must be worked in worsted, and hung up in all the New York clubs, like 'God bless our home!' and 'Merry Christmas!'"

"I much prefer hearts to clubs, for a steady trump," I remarked.

"You play billiards, I presume?"

" Yes," I innocently replied.

" What 's your average run ? "

It was a tempting bait she shoved under my nose, but I realised the trap; . and was too wary to be caught. " Oh, four, when I 'm in good form."

" Really ? "

" Really."   I did not choose to add that I was talking of the balk-line game, not caring to be too technical with a woman.

" That 's very curious ! " she exclaimed.

" I suppose some devoted friend of mine has told you I 'm only a billiard-marker ? " I inquired.

" No — but — "

" But ? "

" Nothing."

" George Washington became President by always telling the truth."

" That 's the advantage of being a woman," replied Kate. " We don't have to scheme and plot and crawl for the Presidency."

" How about spring bonnets ? " I mildly insinuated.

"Does your mother have a very bad time persuading you to pay for hers?" laughed Kate, mischievously.

I did n't like the question, though I knew she was only teasing, so I recurred to my question. "You have n't told me what that 'nothing' was," I persisted.

"I ought n't," urged Kate.

"Then I know you will," I said confidently.

"Well, Seymour Halsey said to Weedon the other night, 'I wish you could play with Jack Pellew, so as to knock some of his airs out of him!'"

"Why," I ejaculated, "I could play cushion caroms against your brother's straight game and beat him then!"

"I never did believe that story about George Washington," asserted Kate, with a singular want of relevance.

"No woman could," I answered, squaring accounts promptly.

Here I saw the little preliminary flutter among the ladies, and knowing that I should never speak to Kate again, I said:

"Miss Cortelyou, I'm afraid an unkind remark of mine a little while ago gave you pain. You've probably forgotten it already, but I never shall cease to regret I made it."

"Don't think of it again," she replied, kindly, as she rose. "And thank you for a pleasant evening."

"Don't blame me for that," I pleaded hastily. "It was your own fault."

"Not entirely," denied Kate. "We did it so well that I'm prouder than ever of the family."

"I decline to share this honour with my grandfather," I protested indignantly. "He couldn't keep his temper, bother him!"

We were at the door now, and Kate gave me the prettiest of parting nods and smiles.

"Wasn't it a pity?" she sighed. That was distinctly nice of her. Just like a Cortelyou woman.

"Whew! Jack," whistled Ferdie Gallaudet. "I thought I should die, and expected to sit on your body at the post-mortem." Ferdie thinks he's clever!

"Oh, shut up, Ferdie," I growled, dropping back into my seat.

"Don't wonder your temper's queered," persisted the little ass. "'Wotinell' did you talk about?"

"Family matters," I muttered.

"Oh, I say, that's a bit shiny at the joints. It was too well done to have verged on that subject."

"We talked family matters, and enjoyed it," I insisted.

"Ever hear of George Washington?" inquired Ferdie.

"Kate mentioned him to me to-night, and I promised to put him up at the Knickerbocker for a month."

"Kate!" exclaimed Ferdie.

I lighted my cigar.

"Kate!" he repeated, with a rising inflection. "Now look here, I wasn't born yesterday."

"Where's your family Bible?" I inquired blandly.

"You'll be saying next that to-night's arrangement was by 'special request.'"

"You were across the table," I retorted. "Draw your own conclusions."

"I suppose you'll join her later," suggested Ferdie, in an irritating manner.

I wouldn't be bluffed by him, so I replied pointedly, "I may, to save her from worse."

"Give you odds on it," offered Ferdie.

"I don't make bets where women are concerned," I crushingly responded.

"Sorry the strain has left you so bad-tempered," said Ferdie, rising. "There's Caldwell beckoning to me. Ta, ta!"

I have liked Caldwell ever since.

When we joined the ladies I went over to Kate.

"This is persecution," she smilingly protested, as she made room for me on the sofa.

"I know it," I cheerfully groaned, as I sat down beside her. "But I had to for the sake of the family."

"A family is a terrible thing to live up to!" sighed Kate.

"Terrible!" I ejaculated.

"Fortunately it will only be for a moment," she assured me.

"If you go at once," I urged, "they'll all think it's the feud."

"What a nuisance!" cried Kate. "I ought to be on my way to a musical this very minute."

"On the principle that music hath charms?" I queried.

"Good-night!" she said, holding out her hand. I had already noticed what pretty hands Kate had.

"Forgive me!" I begged.

"Never!" she replied.

"You are serious?" I questioned, and she understood what I meant as if I had said it. I do like people who can read between the lines!

She amended her "never" to, "Well, not till I have had my chance to even the score."

"Take it now."

"I have n't time."

"I will submit to anything."

" My revenge must be deep."

" I will do the thing I most hate."

" Even afternoon teas ? " laughed Kate, archly.

I faltered in voice while promising, " Even afternoon teas ! "

" Then I 'll send you a card for mine," she ended, and left me, crushed and hopeless.

* *
*

No. That did n't end the feud. It only led to a truce. For a time things went very well, but then the quarrel broke out with renewed force. You see, Kate claimed I spoiled the boy, and I claimed she did the spoiling. So we submitted it to arbitration. My mother said Kate was very judicious, and her father declared I was a model parent. Then we called in his godmother, and she decided we all four spoiled him. It 's been open war ever since, with an occasional brief cessation of hostilities whenever Kate kisses me. After the boy 's grown up, I suppose, peace will come again.

His godmother? Oh! Mrs. Baxter. You see, we could n't do less, for she had talked it all over town that the match was of her making. Her making! In ten cases out of nine she would have had a disrupted dinner. It's lucky for her that Kate was a Cortelyou woman!

"THE BEST LAID PLANS"

AS ENACTED

IN

Two Social Cups of Tea,
Two Social Jokes, and
One Social Agony.

SCENE

Parlour in country house of Mrs. Wycherly.

CHARACTERS

MRS. WYCHERLY,	LORD FERROL,
MISS HELEN WYCHERLY,	GEORGE HAROLD,
MISS ROSE NEWCOME,	STEVEN HAROLD,
MISS AMY SHERMAN,	DENNIS GRANT.

SYLLABUS

ACT I

A cup of tea and two social jokes.
5.30 P. M. Friday.

ACT II

A cup of tea and one social agony.
5.30 P. M. Tuesday.

ACT I

SCENE. — *Parlour in country house with doors r. and l. At back, a fireplace with open fire. Down centre l., a small table, with white blotting-pad, large paper-knife, and writing paraphernalia; and two chairs r. and l. Down centre r., a small table with tea-service, and chair r. At extreme r. two easy-chairs.*

MRS. WYCHERLY sits at writing-desk r. with teacup on table, reading a letter in her hand. AMY sits at desk l. HELEN at tea-table, making tea. STEVEN at mantel. GEORGE and DENNIS seated at r. with teacups.

Helen. Another cup, mama?

Steven. She does n't hear you, Helen.

George. Thanks to *his* precious letter.

Helen (louder). More tea, mama!

Rose (outside l., calling). Are you having tea, Helen?

Helen Yes, Rose.

Amy. And something very exciting as well.

George. More exciting even than your novel, I 'll be bound.

Dennis (*calling*).   Bring the chocolates
with you, if you have n't eaten them all.

Enter Rose, *l., with box of chocolates and
book.*

Rose.   What is it?
Dennis.   Ask Mrs. Wycherly.
Rose.   What is the excitement, Mrs.
Wycherly?
George.   Louder.
Amy (*loudly*).   Mrs. Wycherly!
Mrs. W. (*starting*).   Oh!   What?
George.   That is just the problem.   Is
he a what, or is n't he?
Dennis (*bitterly*).   I don't believe it will
make the least difference even if he proves
a " What is it."
Steven (*more bitterly*).   No, we fellows
see how it will be!   The moment " me lud "
arrives, we shall be nowhere with you girls.
George.   George Augustus Guelph Dun-
stan, Earl of Ferrol and Staunton!   His
very letter of acceptance has made Helen
forget that it is cream — not sugar — that
I " omit for want of space."

Helen. Not at all! If you had been polite you would have given that cup to Rose. As for his lordling, do you for an instant suppose that I intend to compete as long as Rose and Amy are here? No, sir — I leave him to my betters, *D. V.*

Mrs. W. Well, really, I don't think that either his titles or his being in the hands of an oculist is any excuse for making his time so indefinite (*looks at letter*). He will be charmed to pay me a visit, " by next Friday, or perhaps even sooner." Now is n't that a nice position to leave a hostess who wishes to make his stay quite as pleasant as his papa made mine when I was at the " Towers." Imagine this betitled being getting into the Junction by the evening train and then having to walk over to Beechcroft.

Rose. Oh, would n't it be lovely to see him coming in at the gate, so wet and muddy that Tiger would make the same mistake that he did with that poor minister?

Dennis. I hope, if he does have to foot

it, he will not bring the usual number of
parcels that the swells on the other side
consider as necessary as those books which
Charlie Lamb said " no gentleman should
be without."

Amy. Mrs. Wycherly, how can this
man be two earls at once ?

Steven. The English aristocracy finds
it convenient to have an alias now and
again.

Mrs. W. I 'm not sure, Amy, but I believe it has something to do with his
mother. I never could understand the
peerage.

George. Ye gods! to think of a mother
with a marriageable daughter not under-
standing the peerage !

Helen. I won't be slandered by you.
Marriageable daughter, indeed !

Rose (scornfully). Yes, is n't that a regular man's view of it ?

Dennis. Well, I think it 's very credit-
able to be without a peer.

Amy. That depends on how you appear.

Rose.   And that depends on your *appear age.*

George (pityingly).   Don't notice them ; they're quite harmless.   Speaking of the peerage, though, did any of you see Labouchere's screed in " Truth "?

Mrs. W.   I have n't, for one — what was it ?

George.   Bass, the proprietor of the pale ale, has just been made a baron, and this was an editorial on the " Last Addition to the Beerage."

Amy.   Mrs. Wycherly, do let me have the letter: I want to see what kind of a hand he writes.

[Mrs. W. *passes letter to* Amy.

Dennis.   There! That's the way in this life.   I'll be bound you never wanted to see what my writing was like.

Rose.   Well, did you ever want to see Amy's hand ?

Steven.   Hers is too small to make it worth while.

Amy (sweetly).   *Is* your tea sweet enough, Steven ?

Dennis. Why waste your sweetness on the desert air?

Steven. Thank you, Dennis, but I am not a deserted heir, and don't suppose I shall be, till The Right Honourable George Augustus Guelph Dunstan, Earl of Ferrol and Staunton, puts in his appearance. Till then, Mrs. Amy Sherman Micawber will never desert her Steven.

Helen. Really, I think it is very unkind to say all these things before Lord Ferrol arrives. If you begin like this over the "cheerful and uninebriating teacup," with a good dinner not far distant, what will you say when you have just dragged yourself out of bed to breakfast?

Dennis (fiercely). The talking point will be passed. We shall act! Bul-lud!!!

George (rising and setting teacup on tea-table). So let it be understood, if you girls give us the cold shoulder when his lordship arrives, we will not be responsible for the consequences.

Steven. But don't say we did n't warn you.

Helen. Well, you deserve to have the cold shoulder for talking to us so.

Rose. Yes, just as if we had all turned tuft-hunters.

Mrs. W. At least it shows modesty. The boys all take for granted they cannot stand up against the new-comer.

Rose. Oh, Mrs. Wycherly, what nice, honest, guileless men you must have known when you were a girl! To think that *these* should gain the reputation of modesty by their grumbling!

Helen. Yes, dear, they are delusions and snares, having fully mastered Talleyrand's aphorism " that words were meant to conceal ideas."

Amy. "Put not your trust in kings and princes."

George. That's just what we want, only please extend it to the aristocracy.

Rose. You all deserve to have us leave you to your own devices, as soon as we can get a decent substitute.

Mrs. W. Well, if Lord Ferrol is anything like his father, I can promise you no unworthy one, even compared to *my* boys here.

Steven (crossing down stage to Mrs. W. and bowing). Mrs. Wycherly, the race does not improve. Why are the daughters no longer as their mothers were?

Helen.
Amy. } Oh!!!
Rose.

Helen (springing to her feet). Mr. Chairman, or Mrs. Chairwoman, is not the honourable gentleman's language unparliamentary?

Rose. It's uncomplimentary, and I believe that is what unparliamentary generally means.

Amy (rising). I move the expulsion of the honourable gentleman.

Helen (rising). Second the motion.

Omnes. Question! Question! Question!

Mrs. W. (rising with mock solemnity and leaning on desk). Gentlemen, after the *most mature* deliberation the speaker must announce three decisions. First, the language was not uncomplimentary, and —

Rose ⎫   ⎫ Bribery!
Helen ⎬ *together.* ⎬ Treachery, treachery!
Amy ⎭   ⎭ Oh! Oh! Oh!!

Mrs. W. (pounding on table with paper-knife). Order! Order! — And *ergo*, not unparliamentary. Secondly, that in consequence the motion of expulsion is not in order. Thirdly, even if it were in order, the question could not be taken without debate.

Rose. I appeal to the House.

Dennis (rising). All right! Three to three. Speaker throws casting vote with us. How do you do — minority? [*Bows.*

Helen (rising). Excuse me. We three decline to vote, so there is no quorum. The question is before the House still, and can be spoken to.

Dennis. How badly the question must feel.

Amy. Not half so badly as you ought to.

Mrs. W. (pounding). Order! The dignity of the chair must be upheld!

Rose. Then why don't you hold it up?
We 've no objection.

Amy (rising). Mr. Speaker —

Mrs. W. The   honourable   member
from — from —

George. Philadelphia?

> [*Passes* AMY *the chocolates from
> tea-table.*

Amy (sinking faintly into chair). Oh,
not so bad as that!

Mrs. W. Very well — from the slough
of despair —

Amy. Mr. Speaker, I rise from my
slough of despair to demand, with a tear
in my eye —

Dennis. And a chocolate in your
mouth —

Mrs. W. (pounds). Order! —

Amy. To vindicate myself —

George. Well, if you 're going to rise,
why don't you do it?

*Mrs. W. (crossing to tea-table, and seizing
hot water pot.)* I shall pour the hot water
on the next person who interrupts the
honourable gentleman.

Amy. To vindicate myself and my compeers in the — alas! — opposition. We have remained silent under the slur of malice — we have watched the arbitrary and — (I fear corrupt is an unparliamentary word) — ah — questionable rulings of the presiding officer. But, so saith the adage, " Even the worm will turn ; " and why not woman ? So when we hear the distinguished and courteous stranger, about to enter our sacred portals, maligned and sneered at — then — then do we turn upon the " allegators " and declare, that as soon as the shadow of his " gracious " — no — I mean " early " presence darkens these halls of misrule, then, with one accord, for better, for worse, we will cleave to him.

Feminine Omnes. We will.

Rose. Now, boys, you see what you have done ! and, as you remarked a moment ago, " Don't say we did n't warn you."

[*Bell rings.*

Mrs. W. There, young people, — that is the dressing bell. Now don't loiter, for I shall frown on any one who is not in the drawing-room five minutes before seven. I declare this sitting adjourned.

> [*All rise.* MRS. W. *crosses back and exits r. d.* ROSE *comes down c. and whispers to* AMY; *they laugh, put their hands behind each other's waists, and skip up r.*

Rose and Amy (*singing*). "Johnny, get your gun, get your sword, get your pistol. Johnny, get your gun, get your gun, get your gun."

> [*Exit r. d. Men all laugh heartily.*

Helen (*rapping on table in imitation of Mrs. W.*). Order! Order!

George. Cash!

> [*Men all laugh.* HELEN *looks at them scornfully and then exits r. d.* DENNIS *starts to follow.*

George. What's your hurry, Dennis? Lots of time.   [*Sits.*

Steven (*reseating himself*). I bless my governing star every night that it was given to my sex to dress in the time spent by t'otherest in doing up its back hair.

Dennis (crossing back to fireplace). Oh, yes! But as one girl said to me, " That time is n't worth having, for you can't be with us ! "

George. You must both have been pretty far gone, old fellow.

Dennis. Not half so badly as the girls are prospectively on "me lud."

Steven. No, we are in for "a bad quarter of an hour " when he shows up.

Dennis. If he will only prove a show !

Steven (sadly). The only English swells I 've met were very jolly, gentlemanly fellows.

Dennis (cheerfully). All the more chance that this one turns out the delicate little wood violet, such as we occasionally read of in the papers as ornamenting the " Ouse of Lords."

George (gloomily). I am afraid we shall be the flower part of this show.

Dennis. In what respect ?

George. Why, wall flowers, of course.

Steven. Really, it 's no joking matter. I don't know how long the girls will carry on their intended neglect, but it will be strong while it lasts.

Dennis (*coming down stage indignantly*). If I have to put in two days of life without — without —

Steven. (*interrupting*). Faith, hope, or charity, which ?

George. Why don't you say Amy, and have done with it ?

Dennis (*half turning*). Very well. If I have to put in a week here, ten miles from anything, with Amy overflowing with sweetness for that — that — [*Hesitates.*

George. Oh, speak it out, old man ! The word will do you good.

Dennis. No, it would n't do justice to the subject.

Steven. Well, Dennis, you need n't think you 're the only one in this box.

Dennis. Hope he 'll get here on a rainy night, and no carriage at the station, as Rose suggested. Do you suppose a fiver would make our dearly beloved Burgess misunderstand the carriage order ?

George. Burgess is a living proof of

the saying, that "every man has his price."

Steven.   How do you know?

George.   I found it out when he drove Mrs. Wycherly home, quite forgetting to say that Rose and I were to be picked up at Oakridge, as she had specially directed.

Steven (*reprovingly*).

> "You sockin' old fox!
> You pretty white cat—
> I sink dear mama
> Should be told about dat."

Dennis (*sadly*).   It might be possible to corrupt the worthy Burgess, but, unless we could arrange for a rainy day, I don't see that it would do us much good.   The Anglo-Saxon does n't think much of ten miles.

Steven.   No; and the Wycherlys would be so hurt at a guest of theirs having such an accident that they would be doubly sweet to him.

Dennis.   What day did he say he would come?

Steven. " Friday, or perhaps sooner."

George. I suppose the " D. & T." can 't arrange one of their numerous accidents for that train ?

Dennis (*crossly*). Of course not ! Whoever heard of a timely railroad disaster ?

George. Oh, for a mishap of some kind !

Steven (*springing to his feet and slapping his leg*). Fellows, I have an inspiration !

George. Did you get it by inheritance, or out of a bottle ?

Steven. Look here ; his ludship does not arrive, probably, till Friday. My friend, Frank Parker, is to come up here Tuesday. Let's make him personate the " Lord high everything else."

George ⎱ *together* ⎰ Well ?
Dennis ⎰   ⎱ What for?

[*Both rise and come down stage to* STEVEN.

Steven. Why, in the first place, we shall fool the girls. That 's one for us ! In the second place, they 'll carry out their tender programme on him, and so be tired of it when the "only genuine has our name blown in the bottle" puts in his appearance. That's two for us! Thirdly and lastly, we will tell him to be a snob, so that the girls will find it impossible to carry out their plans on him. That's three for us!

Dennis. But will Parker dare to play such a trick in his first visit? Would n't he be like those would-be tragedians whose first and last appearances are identical?

Steven. Oh, Mrs. Wycherly would forgive him anything, for he is the son of an old sweetheart of hers. As for Frank, he's up to anything, and has lived so long in the West that his highest form of amusement is a practical joke.

Dennis. But how are you going to fool our hostess?

George. Why, she has never seen Frank, and only heard of his existence when Steven and I brought word of the jolly fellow we had met in Colorado.

Steven. And, besides, he's a winner in disguising his person and voice. George and I coached all one day, lamenting that he had been left behind, and there he was, sitting beside the driver all the time. Now to the act!

[*Goes to writing-table, and writes. After writing a page, he blots it on blotter and turns over and writes on second sheet.*

Dennis. If it works I don't go back to the city by a long sight. The governor may go it alone till I have seen the fun.

George (*rising and imitating English accent and using his watch as an eye-glass*). I say, Steve, cawnt he make the heavy English noticeable?

Dennis. Yes; tell him to come out strong on that.

George. And remember he's in the hands of an oculist, doncher know. That will be a good excuse for goggles.

Dennis. Tell him we'll share the expense if he will only come.

Steven. What was his third name?

George. George Augustus Guelph Dunstan — otherwise Dust-pan.

Dennis.   When is an earl a small thing?

George (with disgust).   He never is, when he's in this country.

Dennis.   You never could guess a conundrum!

George.   Give it up, old man.

Dennis.   When he's a little early.

George.   Hurry up, Steve. Dennis is in sad need of dinner.

Steven (reading letter).   How's this?

"Dear Frank, — We hear you are to come up here on Tuesday. Now, if you want a soft thing pay heed to what I write. We expect a howling English Lord up here the last of the week, and the girls are going to lay themselves out for his benefit, just to spite us poor republicans. Put on goggles, a beard and wig; get a big pattern suit and a leather hat-box, and telegraph Mrs. Wycherly (in the name of Ferrol), that you will arrive on the 5.15 train Tuesday. You will be met, coddled, caressed, etc. etc., till we shall all call you tenderfoot. But a word in your ear! Make yourself rather disagreeable. Dress in the wrong clothes at meals. Use the words 'nasty' and 'beastly' frequently, and of all things meet the girls more than half-way in their attentions. Your name is George Augustus Guelph Dunstan, Earl of Ferrol and Staunton. Your papa is the Marquess of D-a-c-h-a-n-t (pronounced Jaunt). Your dear mama is no more. You have been in Florida, where you hurt your eyes, and are just from Washington — 'a beastly bore, you know.' I would give untold gold if I could do it instead of you.

     "Always yours,   Steve."

Dennis. I say, boys, we must have a kodak ready for the unveiling, and catch the girls' faces on the fly.

George ⎫
Steven ⎬ (*together, shaking hands and laughing heartily*). Oh! won't
Dennis ⎭ it be rich!

    Enter Rose, *r. d.*

Rose (*crossing up stage to r.*). Why, you wretched boys, have n't you gone up yet?
  [*Men jump and turn with consternation.*

Steven (concealing letter behind him).
Why — ah — is it late?

Enter HELEN, *r. d., and crosses to tea-table,
which she draws back to l.*

Rose. Late! You've just ten minutes
to dress. Be quick! Mrs. Wycherly has
been stopped in the hall by a telegram,
and if she catches you here you'll never
hear the last of it.

[*Men exit hurriedly and awkwardly l. d.*

Helen. Talk of the tardiness of
women!

Rose. I know they've been talking
about us. Did you see how guilty they
looked?   [*Crosses to desk.*

Enter AMY, *r. d.*

Amy. After what Mrs. Wycherly said
of tardiness, they ought to look guilty.

*Rose (seating herself at desk and arrang-
ing pens, etc.).* If they are not late, it's
Seymour's fault, not theirs.

Helen. I hope mama won't wait for
them. I have a good mind to tell Seymour to put a lump of ice in the soup.

Amy. I should rather see those good for-nothing, gossiping, over-spoiled men there.

[*Rose begins to study blotter with great interest.*

Helen. They deserve some kind of penance for their behaviour this afternoon.

Amy. Yes, even in addition to our intended neglect when Lord Ferrol arrives.

Helen. Oh, we can make it a capital joke, and if Lord Ferrol is only nice we can have both the joke and a good time.

Amy. Well, I don't care what Lord Ferrol is; I am going to use him to punish — them.

Helen. Oh! Amy, why that significant pause? We all know how them spells his name.

Rose (springing to her feet with a scream). Girls! Girls!!

Amy (startled). What's the matter?

Rose (melodramatically). My Lords!

My Lords! There are traitors in the camp and treachery stalks rampant.

[*Comes to centre with blotter.*

Helen. Oh, come off that roof!

Rose. No, really, I'm in dead earnest.

Amy. What is it, Rose?

Rose (*evidently reading with difficulty from blotter*). Listen. " Dear Frank,—We hear you are to come up here on Tuesday. Now, if you want a soft thing, pay heed to what I write—" Oh, I can't read it backwards. Where is a mirror?

Helen (*rushing to mantel*). Here, Here.

[*Holds mirror in front of blotter.*

Rose (*reading*). "We are expecting a howling English Lord up here the last of the week, and the girls are going to lay themselves out for his benefit."

Helen }
Amy } (*with intense anger*). What!!!

Rose (*reading*). " Just to spite us poor republicans. Put on goggles, a beard and wig; get a big pattern suit and a leather hat-box. Telegraph Mrs. Wycherly (in the name of Ferrol) that you will arrive on

the 5.15 train Tuesday.   You will be met,
coddled, CARESSED !!

       [*Drops blotter in rage.*

Amy (*shrieking*).   Oh!

Helen (*intensely*).   What!!   (*Grabs at blotter eagerly*)   Here, you read too slowly, let me.   (*Amy holds mirror.*)   " Coddled, caressed, till we shall call you tenderfoot. But a word in your ear!   Make yourself rather disagreeable.   Dress in the wrong clothes at meals.   Use the words ' nasty ' and ' beastly ' frequently, and of all things meet the girls half-way in their attentions. Your name is George Augustus — "   It ends there.

      [*Girls look at each other indignantly.*

Amy (*dangerously*).   It was about time!

      [*Going to the mantel and replacing
        mirror.*

Helen.   What shall we do?

Amy.

  " And he said can this be?
    We are ruined by Chinese cheap labour (*pause*)
    We will go for them heathen Chinee."

Helen (*turning*).   Yes! — but how?

Amy. Girls, put on your thinking-caps, and hunt for some terrible punishment.

Rose. Something " lingering, with boiling oil or melted lead."

Enter MRS. W. *r. d., with telegraph blank in hand.*

Mrs. W. Why, girls, what were those shrieks about ?

Rose (with embarrassment). Oh, nothing, Mrs. Wycherly. That is —

Amy. I hope we did n't frighten you, Mrs. Wycherly.

Mrs. W. Oh, no ! I was only coming in to speak to Helen. (*Helen comes to centre.*) I have just received a despatch from Frank Parker. He has been called back to San Diego by the illness of his mother, so we shall not have his visit after all. (*Hands telegram to* HELEN *and sits at desk r.* ROSE *sits at desk l.* HELEN *and* AMY *cross to r. and evidently consult over telegram.*) I really am very sorry, for I wanted to renew with the son a very old family friendship, but there is no chance, for he has gone West already.

Helen (crossing to Mrs. W. and pleading). Oh, mama! Will you not keep it a secret from the boys? Only George and Steven would care, and we have a really good reason for not wanting them to know. Oh, please, mama!

[*Puts arms round* MRS. W *'s. neck.*

Amy (beseechingly). Oh, Mrs. Wycherly, please do!

Rose (kneeling imploringly). Do, Mrs. Wycherly!

Mrs W. (suspiciously). What mischief are you concocting now? (*rising and going to l. d., followed by all the girls*). Well, I won't promise not to, but I will hold my tongue till I see that I had better speak.

Helen. Oh, you dear mama!

Mrs. W. (laughing). Temper your justice with mercy.   [*Exits l. d.*

Helen (melodramatically coming down c.). Who talks to me of justice and mercy!

Rose. Helen, can't you arrange to

have Burgess drive over to that 5.15 train? It would be so lovely to see the men's faces when the carriage came back empty.

Amy. Gracious! If we only could get the real Ferrol here, in place of the fictitious, and yet make the men think it was Mr. Parker.

Rose. But Lord Ferrol won't be here till Friday, and by that time the boys will have either found it out, or suspect from the time that it really is the genuine article.

Amy. I.'ll tell you what to do. Let me wire my cousin Jack Williams to get himself up as an Englishman, and come up here on Tuesday. I can coach him so that he can pass himself off for Mr. Parker, and the two are enough alike, judging from the description, if disguised, to fool the boys.

Helen. But the moment they were alone with him they would find —

Rose (interrupting). We 'll arrange it so that until we are ready for developments, they shall have no chance to find out.

Rose. But how about Mrs. Wycherly? She knows Mr. Williams, does n't she?

Amy. We 'll let her into the secret — she'll enjoy it as much as any of us.

Helen. And she 's always wanted to have your cousin here.

Rose. Quick, Amy. Write the telegram.

    [*All rush to desk.* AMY *sits in chair l.*

Helen. Mercy! but you 'll ruin yourself with such a one.

Rose. We 'll have to share the expense.

Amy (*getting paper and pencil*). No, I shall only send a short despatch, and write full particulars by letter. Let me see — (*Aloud.*) " Come up here disguised as an Englishman — goggles, beard, wig, loud clothes — "

Rose. And hat-box.

Amy. " And hat-box, by the train that gets here? — " [*Looks at* HELEN *inquiringly.*

Helen. Five fifteen.

Amy. "That gets here at 5.15 Tuesday. Wire Mrs. Wycherly in name of Ferrol that you will be here at that time. Further particulars by post, but don't fail. — Amy."   [*Rises and folds telegram.*

Rose. If he will only come! Think of those boys watching our attention to him, and laughing in their sleeves.

Rose. And we all the time laughing at them.

Helen. And think of their faces when the discovery is made!

Rose. Oh, Helen! You must have your camera ready, and take them at that moment.   [*All laugh.*

CURTAIN

ACT II

SCENE. — *Same room, and same arrangement, except that tea-table is up back to r., and the easy-chair l. is down centre.* MRS. W. *sits chair c. sewing.* ROSE *sits on arm of easy-chair r.* AMY *walking up and down at back.* HELEN *sits chair r. of fireplace.*

Amy (restlessly). I am so excited I can't keep still. If Jack had n't tele-graphed when he did, I could never have survived the nervous strain — but were n't the men's faces lovely when you read the dispatch at luncheon! Sly dogs!

Helen. I hope it will take the boys so long to clear the snow off Silverspoon that we can have your cousin alone for a few minutes.

Rose. No such luck as that! Our evening's skating will hardly weigh with them, compared to the danger of our greeting the supposed Mr. Parker without their moral support to carry him through.

Helen. I almost wish it were Mr. Parker instead of Mr. Williams who is coming. How we could torture them all by awkward questions!

Rose. I don't think I ever appreciated before how deliciously the Indian must feel when he takes his enemy's scalp.

Mrs. W. Why, you blood-thirsty little wretch!

Helen. Mama, we must make our arrangements so that they will have no chance to interview him this evening. Then, to-morrow, we will either fully coach him, or let them find out the trick — according to our wishes.

Mrs. W. Let me see, — I will meet him at the front door; the moment the carriage drives up —

Helen. Yes, and you must bring him in here to tea. We won't let him go till the bell rings for dressing. Then we will all see him upstairs.

Mrs. W. But you can't watch him after he is once in his room, and any of the men can go to him.

Rose. "Not if the court understand himself, and he thinks he do." We will spell each other, so that one of us shall sit in the upper hall till Mr. Williams comes downstairs. The boys would never dare to run such a battery without a better excuse than they can invent for going to the room of an entire stranger.

Mrs. W. That makes it safe till we leave them to their cigars.

Helen (*coming down, and sitting on the arm of Mrs. W.'s chair*). Mama, you will have to tell the boys that for a particular reason, cause unspecified, you want to let the servants clear the dining-room early, so as to set them free. Tell them to smoke in the library; we will sit with them and put up with the smoke for once.

Rose. That will do, and you must break up the party at our usual bed-time with the excuse that Lord Ferrol, after his journey, will want to retire early. Take no denial, and we will escort him upstairs. Then we girls will sit on the divan in the hall and gossip till we feel sure that all is safe.

Amy.   And we 'll write a note making an early appointment with him in the valley summer house; and then — (*Sounds of laughter outside.*)   Hush!

Enter GEORGE, STEVEN, *and* DENNIS, *r. d., and cross over to fireplace, where they stand and warm their hands.*

Mrs. W.   Ah, what a breath of winter freshness you bring in with you!

Steven.   It is a simply glorious after-noon.   How you girls could stay indoors and roast over a fire is a puzzle to me!

Dennis.   You forget, Steve, that tele-gram which came at luncheon.   They were afraid they might lose a few moments of his society!

George.   If his ludship is n't afraid of a little frost, we will show him how to spend an evening on the ice.

Dennis.   I 'll bet a box of chocolates that he does n't know how to skate.   (*Aside to men.*)   They don't have ice in Southern California.

Amy.   Ten pounds and taken.   (*Aside to girls.*)   Jack is a superb skater !

Steven.   Two to one that Dennis wins.

Rose.   I suppose you think you are betting on a certainty, so I shall take you up, just to make you feel ashamed when I lose.

Steven.   Mrs. Wycherly, can't we have our tea without waiting for his giblets?   I am simply famished!

Helen (*crossing to l.*).   I wonder if men ever really think of anything besides eating.

George.   If you think that clearing the drifts off that lake is a light and ornamental position under the government, try it.

Mrs. W. (*rising and reseating herself at desk chair r.*).   Well, Helen, you may make it now, only save a cup for Lord Ferrol.

> [GEORGE *pulls easy-chair c. back to r., while* DENNIS *and* STEVEN *bring tea-table to former position by chair.* ROSE *exits l. d.*

Helen (*coming to tea-table and holding cup up*).   Lord Ferrol's cup.

Steven.   Oh, no!

Dennis.   Never!

[*They try to obtain possession of it. Helen (going round table and sitting, still holding cup).*   Not for you.

Enter ROSE *with hot water pot. Men return to fire-place.* AMY *sits easy-chair l. of tea-table.*

Rose (rubbing teapot against Dennis's hand as she passes).   Hot water.

Dennis (jumping and looking at his hand).   Not the least doubt of it.

Helen.   Make the most of it, boys: it's the last time our tea will be sweet to you!

Dennis.   Why is Helen like a " P. & O." steamer?

Helen (indignantly).   I'm not!

Steven.   Because she's steaming the tea?

Dennis.   No.

Amy.   Don't keep us in suspense.

Steven.   Because she's full of tease.

George.   You make me tired.

Steven.   Is that why you sat down so often on the ice?

Helen.   Is n't that just like George, —
sitting round, while the rest do the
work.

George.   If you think there 's any particular pleasure in sitting in a snowdrift,
there 's one outside, right against the
verandah.

Steven.   That would never do at present.
It might result in a cold, and so destroy
our little plan of winning the maiden
affections of — well, I won't give him a
name till I have seen him!

Helen.   It is hard to put up with foreign
titles, but as long as our government will
not protect that industry, the home product
is so rude, *boorish*, VULGAR, and YOUNG,
that we cannot help — "

Rose (interrupting).   Listen! (*Pause.*)
There 's the carriage.

   [*All rise and start toward r. door.*
*Mrs. W. (rising and intercepting them
at door*).   Now, don't all come running out
to frighten the poor man. (*Men return to
fireplace, girls reseat themselves.*)   Let his
first greeting be with me, and then I will

bring him in and let him see you and get a cup of tea. [*Exit r.*

Dennis (*stalking down stage*).

Fe, Fo, Fi, Fum,
I smell the blood of an Englishman;
Be he alive, or be he dead,
I'll grind his bones to make me bread.

Rose (pointing at Dennis).

Ping Wing, the pieman's son,
Was the very worst boy in all Canton,
He stole his mother's —

Mrs. W. (*outside*). No, I'm sure —

Enter MRS. W. *and* LORD F. (*in goggles and wig*) *r. d. and come down c.*

Mrs. W. You are chilled by your ride, so you must have a cup of tea before going to your room. Helen, this is Lord Ferrol. My daughter, Miss Wycherly, Miss Newcome, Miss Sherman, Lord Ferrol —.

Lord F. (*bowing*). Charmed, I assure you!

Mrs. W. My nephews, Mr. George and Steven Harold, and Mr. Grant. There! the formidable host is reviewed, and you can now make yourself as comfortable as possible.

Lord F. Er, thanks, but if you will allow me, I will go to my room first, — I am so filthy.

Mrs. W. Oh, but you really must have tea first.

Lord F. You're awfully good, I'm sure. Er, will you pardon my glasses, but I burned my eyes shooting alligators, and, er! that was why I couldn't make a more positive date, for I was in the hands of an oculist.

Amy (aside). Oh! Jack, what a lie!

Steven (aside). Didn't I tell you the old fellow would come out strong? I shouldn't know him myself?

Amy (rising from easy-chair l.). Here, Lord Ferrol, I have been sitting in the easiest chair to prevent the others from taking it, so that you should have it when you came.

Lord F. Er, thanks, awfully!

[*Sits.* AMY *stands in devoted attitude just at back of his chair.*

Rose (*rising and bringing hassock*).   Let me give you this hassock — one is so uncomfortable in these deep chairs without one.

Lord F.   Er, Thanks!   You're very kind.

Helen (*tenderly*).   Lord Ferrol, will you tell me how you like your tea?

Lord F.   Strong, please, with plenty of cream and sugar.

Amy (*admiringly*).   Ah, how nice it is to find a man who takes his tea as it should be taken! (*looking at men scornfully*).   It is really a mental labor to pour tea for the average man.

Dennis.   Average is a condition common to many; therefore we are common. Yet somebody said the common people were never wrong.

Helen.   Well, they may never be wrong, but they can be uncommonly disagreeable!

Lord F.   Yes, that's very true.   You know, at home we don't have much to do with that class, but out here you can't keep away from them.

Amy (*turning to men*).   There! I hope
you are properly crushed?

Lord F. (*turning to Amy*).   Eh!

Amy (*leaning over Lord F. tenderly*).
Oh, I wasn't speaking to you, dear Lord
Ferrol!

Mrs. W.   I fear that you have had some
unpleasant experiences here, from the way
you speak.

Lord F.   Rather.   (*Helen hands cup
with winning smile.*)   Thanks, awfully!

George.   Perhaps Lord Ferrol will tell
us some of them; we may be able to free
him from a wrong impression.

Lord F.   The awful bore over here is,
that every one tries to make jokes.   Now,
a joke is very jolly after dinner, or when
one goes to " Punch " for it.

Steven.   To what?

Lord F.   To " Punch," don't you know,
— the paper.

Steven.   Oh!   Excuse my denseness;
I thought we were discussing jokes.

Lord F.   I beg pardon?

Amy.   Don't mind him, Lord Ferrol.

George. No, like " Punch," he 's only trying to be humorous.

Lord F. Er, is that an American joke ?

Dennis. I always thought Punch was a British joke !

Lord F. Er, then you Americans do think it funny ?

George. Singularly !

Lord F. What I object to in this country is the way one's inferiors joke. It's such bad form.

Rose (horrified). Surely they have n't tried to joke you ?

Lord F. Yes. Now to-day, coming up here, I took my luggage to the station, and got my brasses, but forgot your direction that it must be re-labelled at the Junction, so they wer'n't put off there. I spoke to the guard, and he was so vastly obliging in promising to have them sent back that I gave him a deem.

Omnes. A what ?

Lord F. A deem — your small coin that 's almost as much as our sixpence, don't you know.

Omnes.   Oh, yes !

Lord F.   Well, the fellow looked at it, and then he smiled, and said loud enough for the whole car to hear : " My dear John Bull, don't you sling your wealth about in this prodigal way.   You take it home, and put it out at compound interest, and some day you'll buy out Gould or Rockefeller."

Helen.   How shockingly rude !   What did you do ?

Lord F.   I told him if he did n't behave himself, I 'd give him in charge.   (*Men all laugh.*)   Now, is   that   another   of your American jokes ?

Dennis (aside).   Oh ! is n't this rich ?

Amy (aside to Lord F.).   Oh, you   are beautiful !

Lord   F.   (bewildered   and   starting). Thanks awfully, — if you really mean it !

Steven (coming   down   to   back   of   Lord F.'s chair).   What   did   she   say, Lord Ferrol ?   You must take Miss Sherman with a grain of allowance.

Amy.   I 'm not a pill, thank you.

Lord F.   Why, who said you were?

Dennis.   Only a homœopathic sugar-plum.

Lord F.   I don't understand.

Steven (*aside to Lord F.*).   Keep it up, old man.   It's superb!

Lord F.   I beg pardon,— did you speak to me?

Steven (*retreating to fireplace*).   Oh, no! only addressing vacancy.

Mrs. W.   I hope, Lord Ferrol, that there has been enough pleasant in your trip to make you forget what has been disagreeable.

Lord F.   Er, quite so.   The trip has been vastly enjoyable.

Rose.   Where have you been?

Lord F.   I landed in New York and spent the night there, but it was such a bore that I went on to Niagara the next day.   From there I travelled through the Rockies, getting some jolly sport, and then went to Florida.

Mrs. W.   Why, you have seen a large part of our country; even more than your

father did. I remember his amazement
at our autumn foliage. He said it was
the most surprising thing in the trip.

Amy. What did you think of it, Lord
Ferrol ?

Lord F. It struck me as rather gaudy.

Rose. Why, I had never thought of it,
but perhaps it is a little vivid.

Dennis (*aside to men*). Oh, how I
should like to kick him !

Steven (*aside to Dennis*). Hush ! You
forget that "Codlin's your friend — not
Short."

George. Did n't you ever see a Vene-
tian sunset ?

Lord F. Oh, yes. Why do you ask ?

George (*sarcastically*). I merely thought
it might be open to the same objection !

Lord F. It might — I don't remember.
I 'll look it up in my journal when I get
home, and see if it impressed me at the
time.

Helen. Do you keep a journal ? (*Rises
and sits on footstool at Lord F.'s feet.*)
How delightful ! (*Beseechingly.*)   Oh,

won't you let me look at what you have with you?

Rose. Please, Lord Ferrol!

Amy. Ah, do!

Lord F. It would bore you, I'm sure.

Dennis (aside). I don't care if he isn't a double-barrelled earl, I should like to kick him all the same!

Helen. Lord Ferrol, you must let us hear some of it.

Rose. If you don't we shall think you have said something uncomplimentary of the American women.

Lord F. No, I assure you I have been quite delighted.

Amy. Then why won't you let us see it?

Lord F. Er, I could n't, you know; but if you really are in earnest, I'll read you some extracts.

Omnes. Oh, do!

Lord F. I ought to explain that I started with the intention of writing a book on America, so this (*producing book*) is not merely what I did and saw, but desultory notes on the States.

Rose.   How interesting !

Lord F.   After your suggestion of what I have written of the American women, I think it best to give you some of my notes on them.

Mrs. W.   By all means !

Lord F. (*reading*).   " Reached Washington, the American capital, and went direct to Mrs. ——. Cabman charged me sixteen shillings. When I made a row, butler sent for my host, who, instead of calling a constable, made me pay the fellow, by insisting on paying it himself. Mr. —— is a Senator, and is seen very little about the house, from which I infer the American men are not domestic — presumably, because of their wild life — "

Mrs. W. (*with anxiety*).   Their what ?

Lord F.   Their wild life, — spending so much of their time on the plains, don't you know.

Mrs. W. (*relieved*).   Oh ! Excuse my misapprehension.

Lord F. (*reading*).   " The daughter is very pretty, which Mrs. —— tells me is unusual in Washington society — as if I could be taken in by such an obvious Dowager puff! (*Men all point at Mrs. W. and laugh. Mrs. W. shakes her finger reprovingly.*) Miss —— says the Boston girls are plain and thin, due to their living almost wholly on fads, which are very unhealthy " (*Speaking.*) I could n't find that word in the dictionary.

Steven. Sort of intellectual chewing-gum, Lord Ferrol.

Dennis. Yes, and like gum, you never get beyond a certain point with it. It 's very fatiguing to the jaw.

Lord F. (*reading*). " She says the New York girls are the best dressed in the country, being hired by the dressmakers to wear gowns, to make the girls of other cities envious, and that this is where they get all the money they spend. Very remarkable! "

Helen. Something like sandwich men, evidently.

Lord F. (*reading*). " The Philadelphia girls, she says, are very fast, but never for long at a time, because the men get sleepy and must have afternoon naps."

Amy. Did she tell you that insomnia is thought to make one very distinguished there?

Lord F. (*making note in book*). Er, thanks, awfully. (*Reading.*) "She says that the Baltimore girls are great beauties, and marry so quickly that there is generally a scarcity. It is proposed to start a joint stock company to colonise that city with the surplus from Boston, and she thinks there ought to be lots of money in it! Another extreme case of American dollar worship! The Western girls, she told me, are all blizzards." (*Speaking.*) I don't think I could have mistaken the word, for I made her spell it. Yet the American dictionary defines blizzard as a great wind or snow storm.

George. That is it, Lord Ferrol. They talk so much that it gives the effect of a wind storm.

Lord F. Ah! much obliged. (*Reading.*) "Went to eight receptions in one afternoon, where I was introduced to a lot of people, and talked to nobody. Dined out somewhere, but can't remember the name. Took in a Miss ——, a most charming and lovely — "

Dennis (interrupting). Ah, there!

Lord F. I beg pardon.

Rose. You must forgive his rude interruption, Lord Ferrol.

Lord F. Oh, certainly! You're sure you're not bored?

Omnes. By no means. Do go on.

Lord F. " A most charming and lovely girl from New York. She thinks Miss —— characterised the cities rightly, except her own. Asked me if I thought she was only a dressmaking advertisement? As scarcely any of her dress was to be seen, I replied that as I could n't look below the table, I was sure it was the last thing one would accuse her of being. She blushed so violently that I had to tell her that I had seen much worse dresses in London; but that did n't please her any better, and she talked to the man next her for the rest of the evening. (*All have difficulty in suppressing their laughter.*) I met a Boston girl afterwards who — "

                         [*Bell rings.*

Mrs. W. Lord Ferrol, there is our summons to the upper regions. We will not make a formal guest of you, but will all guide you to your room. [*All rise.*

Lord F. Er, thanks.

Mrs. W. (*taking Lord F.'s arm*). Your trunks not having arrived (*exit r. d. with Lord F.*) we will none of us —

        [*Exit* AMY *and* HELEN *r. d., evidently laughing.* ROSE *exits l. d. Men all go off into paroxysms of laughter.*

Steven (*suddenly*). Well, I must go and coach him.

Dennis. My dear fellow! you can't paint the lily.

Enter ROSE, *quietly, l. d. Men all check their laughter.*

Rose. I came back for my skates. Why, what are you laughing about! And pray what lily are you going to paint?

George.   My dear cousin, when a person enters a room already occupied, without due warning, she must not ask questions relative to the subject under discussion.

Rose (*talking down stage to conceal her laughter*).   I know very well what you were talking about.   You were making fun of Lord Ferrol.

Steven.   Give you my solemn word we were not making fun of *Lord Ferrol.*

Men.   No!   How suspicious you girls are!

> [*All laugh.*   HELEN *tries to suppress her laughter, and then rushes out r. d., followed by* STEVEN.

Dennis.   That journal was a mighty clever dodge of Parker's.   It staved off all dangerous questions till Steve could coach him.

George.   There were some capital notions in it, too.   If he will only give us a few more risqué anecdotes, none of the girls will dare talk to him.

Dennis.   Did you see Mrs. Wycherly's horrified expression when he alluded to

the wild life of the American men? I am
sure she thought he was going to give us
some "exposures in high life."

Enter STEVEN *hurriedly, r. d.*

Steven. Look here, fellows, you've got
to help me. The girls have planted themselves on the divan upstairs, and I can't
go to Ferrol's room without their seeing
me. Come up and occupy them, while I
slip in.

Dennis. Decoy ducks, eh?

Stuart. That's it. Come along, George.
[*All exit r. d., — slight pause.*

Enter LORD F. *l. d., dressed as before.*

Lord F. (*looking about*). I must have
made a mistake in the door, for I got into
the butler's pantry; but this is right, I am
sure. Queer place and queer manners!
Will make interesting reading, though.
Ah, a good chance to fill up my journal.
(*Seats himself at desk, takes out book, and
writes, speaking aloud and soliloquising as
he does so.*) "At 5.15 reached some unpro-

nounceable and unspellable place.   Was
met by Mrs. Wycherly at front door"—
curious fashion that! It made me take
her for the housekeeper at first.   "She
insisted, in spite of my protests,"— I suppose it was an American idea of hospi-
tality,—"in taking me at once into the
drawing-room and presenting me to the
house-party, and giving me a cup of tea.
I felt very disagreeable, both from the condition I was in, and the fact that all of
them kept making remarks which were
entirely unintelligible to me.   The young
ladies were very kind, but more forward
even than they are in England, though
in a different way."— I confess I rather
liked it.—"Read some of my journal aloud
and had no corrections.   Blizzard applied
to Western girls means that they talk a
great deal.   Was shown to my room by
Mrs. Wycherly and the young ladies,
which was rather embarrassing, especially
as they seemed inclined to linger, and
only hurried out on the appearance of the
gentlemen.   On leaving, one of the girls

slipped her hand into mine and gave it a distinct squeeze, at the same time asking in a whisper, 'Did your sister send her love?'"— Now the idea of Sappho sending her love to a girl of whom she had never heard!—"I pretended not to hear, but she evidently knew that she had been too free, for as she left she jerked her head towards the gentlemen and said, 'They did n't see.' Could not change my travelling suit, my boxes having gone astray. Found a letter pinned to my pin-cushion, and when the valet brought the hot water, he gave me another. Both, judging from the hand-writing and paper, seem to be written by ladies and gentlemen."— I should like to know what they mean? I wonder if it's good form in America to play jokes on guests? (*Produces notes and reads.*) "Dear F."—(*Rises and comes to c.*) Now the idea of the fellow writing to me in that way on the acquaintance of a single afternoon — why, even my best friends only say "Dear Ferrol."—"You were simply marvellous.

I would have staked my bottom dollar on your identity, if I had not known who you were." — Now what does he mean by that, I wonder? — "You were so real that Dennis wanted to kick you, and nothing but the presence of the ladies prevented him." — Gad! I wonder if these fellows can be gentlemen, and if so, whether they are a fair specimen — kick me! (*Pause.*) Well, I suppose they're jealous.— "So don't be too hard on us. Now as to the future. If we do not see each other this evening, you must get up before breakfast, go out of the side door, and strike across the lawn toward the river. Three minutes' walk will bring you in sight of a little summer-house. Come to it, and some of us will be there prepared to instruct you as to yourself, and put you on your guard as to the girls, who, you see, are making a dead set at you." — You know, that's just what I thought. — "Remember, in the bright lexicon, etc., etc., Steve." — Now what does he mean by "bright lexicon?" And does he think I'm going to tramp through the snow, when it's so evidently a joke? (*Opens other note.*) "You dear love of a snob"— Now I should vastly like to know how that is meant. I don't think it's a nice way of beginning a letter, I'm sure. Yet she evidently means it as a compliment — "You were so perfectly delicious that I could scarcely forbear from giving you a kiss."— Extraordinary!— "Indeed I think I will to-morrow, just to make the boys desperate. I only hope your life is insured, for Dennis will probably chuck you out of the window, when I do, and it's too cold for the window to be opened. Fortunately there is plenty of soft snow to break the fall."—Now isn't that a nasty way of joking! One would actually think she enjoyed the prospect of seeing me thrown out the window.—"I have given directions that you are to be called early, and as soon as you can, I want you to come to the valley summer-house. Turn to your right, and walk straight towards the river, and you can't miss it. There you will find a bevy of maidens waiting to metaphorically hug and kiss you, and instruct you so that you may play the part of George Augustus Guelph Dunstan, Earl of Ferrol and Staunton, with sufficient stupidity and vanity. Amy"— Now I should like to know what all that means. (*Reflectively.*) Amy — she's the one who told me I was beautiful the first time she spoke to me. I should like to know what she means!

Enter MRS. W. *r. d.*

Mrs. W. (crossing to c.). Why, I did n't know you had come downstairs, Lord — I hardly know whether to call you Lord Ferrol, but I suppose it is safer.

Lord F. (surprised). Eh?

Mrs. W. (confidentially). I was immensely amused just now in coming down. There are all the boys and girls sitting in the upper hall, each intent on getting a few words with you, or of preventing the others.

Lord F. I suppose I ought to be vastly flattered. Yet I thought the gentlemen disliked me.

Mrs. W. (*laughing*). Oh, they will probably kill you before the end of your visit.

Lord F. Good gracious, Mrs. Wycherly, you 're not speaking seriously!

Mrs. W. You play your part so well that I myself should think that you were to the manner born.

Lord F. (*aside*). I wonder if it is the fashion of the house to speak in innuendoes. (*Aloud.*) Er! Mrs. Wycherly, I am so new to your ways that I should really like to ask you about one or two questions of etiquette. You know that it differs so in countries, and I never want to seem cold or rude. Now, over here, is it customary for young ladies to say that they want to kiss fellows (*voices outside*) who are no relations of theirs?

Mrs. W. Why, I never heard —

Enter all, r. d. HELEN, GEORGE, *and* STEVEN *cross to l.* ROSE *comes down r. to writing-desk.* DENNIS *and* AMY *stand at fireplace.*

Amy (*to Lord F.*).   Oh, here you are! We 've all been waiting upstairs for you.

Lord F.   Er, thanks.

Rose.   I hope we are not late, Mrs. Wycherly.

Mrs. W. (*going up stage to fireplace*). Oh, it does n't matter in the least.   You will simply have grieved Seymour over the dinner.

Rose.   I know I shall grieve him by my appetite.   (*Over desk to Lord F.*)   Why, Lord Ferrol, I am hungry enough to eat you.

Lord F. (*half turning*).   Er, thanks, awfully.   (*Aside.*)   Now, what does she mean?

Amy.   Oh, I would n't eat Lord Ferrol, for you can 't eat your cake and have it. (*Coming down center to Lord F.*)   But I should like to kiss him, if he will let me.

Lord F.   Er, charmed, — if Mrs. Wycherly thinks it proper.

Dennis (*seizing paper-knife from desk and rushing down between them*).   This is too much, Parker!   You are getting more

than your share. (*Turning to Amy.*)
Avaunt, woman! you have raised the sav-
age in me, and behold the consequences!
[*Uses the knife as a scalping knife,
and then tears off* LORD F.'s *wig,
revealing a perfectly bald head.*
Lord F. Gad, sir! what do you mean?
Omnes. Why, who are you?
[AMY *crosses to l. as if bewildered.*
Lord F. Who am I?
Mrs. W. (*with horror*). You are not
really Lord Ferrol?
Lord F. Who else should I be? [*Pause.*
Amy. (*sinking faintly into chair*). And
I asked leave to kiss him!
Mrs. W. (*coming down to c. and speaking
with great anxiety*). Lord Ferrol, my
young people here were each trying to play
a joke on the other, and by a horrible coin-
cidence you have been the victim. (*Im-
ploringly.*) Will you not try to forgive
us now, and let me explain at dinner?
[*All come down stage and seem to
plead.*
Lord F. Well, really, if it's a mistake,

of course I can 't cut up rough. (*To Amy.*)
Then you don 't think I 'm a dear love of
a snob, eh?

Amy (*faintly*). Oh, no, Lord Ferrol.

Lord F. And you don 't want to kiss
me?

Amy (*more faintly*). No, indeed, Lord
Ferrol.

Lord F. Then, Miss Sherman, I will
try to make you do both.

Steven (*coming down c.*). There, did n't
I tell you the real English swells were
very jolly, gentlemanly fellows?

[*Shakes hands with Ferrol.*

Lord F. And did n't I tell you the
Americans were always joking in the wrong
place? (*To Dennis.*) Er, I 'll thank you
for my hair.

CURTAIN

"MAN PROPOSES"

IN

SEVERAL DECLARATIONS

AND

ONE ACT

PLACE
Morning room at the Wortleys.

TIME
After dinner, and before the masked ball.

CHARACTERS

MISS AGNES WORTLEY
(A winner of hearts).

MRS. VAN TROMP
(A widow to be won).

POLLY
(A serving maid who serves).

MR. STUART
(A theoretical bachelor).

MR. REGINALD DE LANCEY VAN TROMP
(A man with ancestors).

MR. CHARLIE NEWBANK
(A man with money).

MR. FREDERICK STEVENS
(A man with neither).

SCENE.—*Morning room in city house,— doors l. and b. Fireplace with fire l. c. Writing-desk, with matches, pens, ink, paper, and hand-bell back centre — chair at desk. Down stage l., easy chair, and an ottoman or light chair c. At extreme down stage r. corner, a bay window, with practical curtains, and a divan seat. On mantel a clock which strikes ten as soon as curtain rises.*

Enter POLLY *l. d.*

Polly (*coming down wearily*). Mercy, how tired I am! And no chance of rest for at least six hours (*drops into chair c.*). Dinners and balls may be fun for those who do the eating and dancing, but it's death on us poor servants. I'm worked hard enough usually, in all conscience' sake, but Miss Agnes has given me just the hardest day I've ever seen! (*Imitates Agnes giving orders.*) "Polly, is my bath ready?"

" Polly, give me my dressing-gown."
" Polly, bring me my coffee." " Now dress
my hair, Polly." " Get me my habit,
Polly." (*Rises.*) " While I 'm in the park,
Polly, sew the ribbons on my two dominos." " Oh, and I 'll be too busy to-day
to write acknowledgments for the bouquets,
Polly, so you may write to Mr. Stevens and
Mr. Van Tromp and Mr. Newbank, and
any others that come, thanking them
for their lovely flowers, which are now
filling my room with sweetness ! " From
seven till eight it's been nothing but " Polly,
do this," and " Polly, do that," and " Where 's
Polly ? " And no one so much as said
" Polly, want a cracker ? " I have n't had a
chance to sit down since I got up. I even
had to eat my dinner off the laundry tubs
(*mimics eating with pen and paper-cutter
at desk*) standing, because the caterers
were everywhere, getting the dinner and
ball supper ready. Miss Agnes says she 's
all " worn out." I wish she could try
my work once in a while. How I should
enjoy telling the rich and sought-after

Miss Agnes Wortley to (*mimicking*) " button my shoes," (*sticks out foot*) or (*waves her hand*) " fetch me my gloves ! " I would give a month's wages if I could only take her place just for to-night at the masked ball. (*Speaking with excitement.*) When she decided that she must have two dominos, so that she could change in the middle of the ball, I thought to myself: 'What's to prevent your slipping on the domino she isn't wearing, and going downstairs ? ' (*Muses.*) If I only dared ! I could easily slip out before she wanted to change ! (*Pause.*) No ! I must n't even think of it or the temptation will be too great.

[*Goes to fireplace, and sitting on rug pokes the fire.*

STUART *appears b. d. and looks in.*

Polly. It would be such fun ! Think of being Miss Agnes for one evening and dancing with all her admirers ! Oh, my ! Supposing one should propose ! Mr. Newbank ! (*Laughs.*) Or Mr. Van Tromp ! (*Laughs again.*) I 'd know what I 'd say to them! Mr. Stevens? I wonder if she cares for him.

Stuart. And how about Mr. Stuart?

Polly (*springing up, flustered*). Oh, Jiminy! Oh — I beg your pardon, Mr. Stuart, I was — I —   [*Hesitates.*

Stuart (*laughing*). Poking the fire, eh? Is this room free territory?

Polly. Yes, Mr. Stuart. It's Miss Wortley's boudoir, but she thought it would be a nice place for people to come when they were tired of dancing downstairs.

[*Courtseys and exits l. d.*

Stuart (*calling out r.*). This way, Fred. Here's a quiet nook saved from the universal ruin and bareness of downstairs.

[*Comes down.*

Enter FRED, *b. d., slowly.*

Stuart. Isn't this luck?

Fred (*gloomily*). There isn't any such thing! Or if there is, I never get any.

Stuart. Now, Fred, you can't say that after this. You and I don't want to stay and smoke with the men. Neither do we want to join the ladies. The other rooms are as bare and uncomfortable as waxed floors and camp-chairs can make them. I suggest trying upstairs, and when I discover and pilot you to this oasis in the desert, you at once begin to grumble.

Fred. I'm sorry I'm bad company, Mr. Stuart; but if I'm so to you, just think what I must be to myself.

Stuart. There is something in that.

Fred. And you only see me occasionally, and I'm with myself day and night.

Stuart (laughing). Pity you can't hire some one to kill your disagreeable companion. I wonder if a jury would n't bring in a verdict of justifiable homicide, if you drowned or hung him.

Fred. I'd like to!

Stuart. Curious. Such a dinner, even when I know it's to be followed by a ball, always puts me in a beatific state of mind.

Fred (wearily). I thought it very long and tedious.

Stuart. And what is worse, you looked it. You looked as glum all through as if you were waiting for the last trump.

Fred (*crossly*). It was n't the last trump I was waiting for. I was —

Stuart (*interrupting*). No, I misworded my sentence. You were waiting for the last of Van Tromp.

Fred. Oh, pshaw!

[*Rises and crosses to r. angrily.*

Stuart (*laughing*). You don't seem to enjoy my pun?

Fred. Oh, if it pleases you, go ahead.

[*Goes up and sits on desk.*

Stuart. Fred, you make a mistake to go into society while you are in this mood. Take a friend's advice and cut it till you are better tempered.

Fred (*impatiently*). I don't go because I enjoy it.

Stuart (*sarcastically*). Ah! You go to make it pleasant for others.

Fred. No, I go because *she* goes.

Stuart (*laughing*). Will you tell me why a woman's reason is always a " because," and a man's is always a " she "?

Fred. *She*'s an excuse for anything!

Stuart. Even for Charlie Newbank?

Fred (rising angrily). Look here, Mr. Stuart, I 'll take a good deal from you; but there is a limit.

Stuart (soothingly). Excuse me, my boy. It is brutal in me, but I am trying to see if I can't laugh you out of it.

Fred (sits chair l. as if discouraged). No use! As they say out West, it 's come to stay and grow up with the country.

Stuart. Oh, I did n't mean your love for Miss Wortley. She 's a sweet, unspoiled girl, in spite of her own and her papa's money, and I hope you 'll win her. I was only trying to cheer you out of your dumps, and make you look at the golden side of things.

Fred. That 's just what I see all the time, and what comes between us. I can't forget her money.

Stuart (springing to his feet). There! That goes to prove a pet little theory of mine, that it is rather hard for a rich girl to marry well.

Fred. I should think you needed a confirmatory evidence.

Stuart. You are just like the rest! You take the conventionally superficial view of it.

Fred. Very well, turn lawyer and argue your case before referee Mr. Frederick Stevens, junior member of the celebrated firm of Mary, Green and Hart.

Stuart. You fire my ambition. Well, (*rising and imitating legal style*) your honour, and gentlemen of the jury, *a priori* and *imprimis* we start with the postulate that the party of the first part, otherwise the girl with money, is usually so spoiled that most fellows won't care for her. But we will leave that out of the argument and say that she is a nice girl. Well, by her parents, her friends, and her reading, she is taught to think that every man who is attentive to her may be a fortune-hunter. The consequence is that she is suspicious, and may say or do something to wound or insult a fellow who cares for her, and so drive him off.

Fred. That's one point for your side.

Stuart. But even if she is not made

suspicious by her money, (*points at Fred*) he is. A decent man dreads to have his motives misjudged. He's afraid that the girl, or her father, or her mother, or her friends, or his friends, will think he is fortune-hunting.

Fred. I should think he did!

Stuart. Finally, her money draws about her a lot of worthless fellows. As a consequence, she is always beset and engaged. You must remember that in this country a man, if he amounts to a row of pins, is a worker, and not a drone. He cannot, therefore, dance the continual attendance that is necessary to see much of a society girl nowadays. This can only be done by our rich and leisured young men, who are few and far between; by foreign titles, who are quite as scarce; and by the idlers and do-nothings, who, if the girl is worth winning, are as distasteful to her as they are to the rest of mortal kind. (*Sits chair c.*) I submit my case.

Fred. Mr. Stuart, you entirely missed your vocation. Allow me to congratulate

you on your *maiden* argument. But at
the same time the referee would call your
attention to the fact that you have failed
to take the relatives into account. They
can overcome all this by heading off
the undesirables and encouraging their
choice.

Stuart. But that's just what they
won't do, and which I don't think they
could to any extent, even if they tried.
How much can Mr. Wortley and Mrs.
Van Tromp control Miss Agnes' compan-
ions at the dinners and dances and other
affairs, which are practically the only places
where she meets men ?

Fred. Here they can.

Stuart. But they don't. You say Mr.
Wortley favours Newbank and Mrs. Van
Tromp encourages her brother-in-law.
Naturally, then, they don't approve your
very evident liking for Miss Agnes. Yet
I see you here quite as often as either of
the favoured ones. Do you think if this
system of exclusion were possible, it would
not have been practised long ago ?

Fred. If you ask it as a conundrum I give it up. But I know that neither of them want me to marry Miss Wortley. Mr. Wortley wishes Newbank's millions to add to the family. Mrs. Van Tromp hopes to graft Miss Wortley on the fine old stock of Van Tromps.

Stuart. And what does the person most concerned want? In this glorious country of ours, where children always know more than parents, the girl's consent is really the only requisite. What does Miss Wortley want?

Fred. I only wish I knew!

Stuart. Well, how does she treat you compared with the other men?

Fred. At first she was very nice and friendly, but latterly she'll have nothing to do with me.

Stuart. A girl of taste!

Fred. I'm in the mood to enjoy such friendly jokes.

Stuart. It was meant kindly, Fred, as you will see in a moment. Now, my boy, I'm going to give you a talking to, and if

14

you resent it, it will only be further con-
firmation of another little theory of mine,
that a man 's an ass who concerns himself
in other people's affairs.

Fred.   Go ahead.   I 'm blue enough to
like anything sour or disagreeable.

[*Sits, desk chair, and leans on desk.*

Stuart.   Now, there at once you give
me the text to preach from.   (*Walks behind chair l. and leans on back, speaking
over it down r.*)   About a year ago a
certain gentleman named Fred meets a
certain lady named Agnes.   We 'll say he
met her at a dance —

Fred.   No, it was yachting.

Stuart.   Ah ! — excuse my lack of his-
torical accuracy.   Well, on a yacht — he
met her; then at a ball — he met her;
then at a cotillion — he met her; then at
a dinner — he met her.   In short, he met
her, and met her, and met her.

Fred (*gloomily*).   Yes, and what is more,
he spent hours trying to.

Stuart.   Well, she was pretty and charming and — I 'm short of an adjective, Fred.

Fred. Of course you are! There is n't one in Webster's Unabridged which would do her justice!

Stuart. That should have been said to her and not wasted on me. Well, we 'll say the girl is plu-perfect. The fellow is rather good looking — eh, Fred?

Fred. I don't know.

Stuart. He talks and dances well; and is, in fact, quite a shining light among her devotees.

Fred (irritably). Oh, cut it, for heaven's sake! [*Rises impatiently.*

Stuart (laughing). Excuse me, — the story-teller never cuts; it 's the editor who does that.

Fred (angrily). Oh, go on.

Stuart. Well, at first this masculine paragon whom I have so meagrely described seems to be doing well. She likes his society and shows it. (*To Fred.*) Right?

Fred. I thought so.

Stuart. But as he gets more interested, he changes. He makes his attentions and feelings too marked — something no girl likes. Then he is cross and moody when she does not give him most of her time and dances. He is inclined to be jealous of every Tom, Dick, and Harry who comes near her, and absurdly tries to dictate what she shall do and not do; which she resents. In short, the very strength of his love makes him an entirely different kind of a man. He is neither companionable nor entertaining; he is both surly and passionate. Do you blame her for repulsing him?

Fred. No, you are right. I know I've given her reason for turning me the cold shoulder.

Stuart. Then if you've known this, why haven't you behaved yourself?

Fred. I've tried to, over and over again; but when I see such cads as Van Tromp and Newbank and the rest of the pack around her, I get perfectly desperate.

Stuart. And why? Now, Van Tromp is not only a fool, which I suppose is the fault of his ancestors, but he is so impecunious that every girl who has money must suspect his motives. Newbank is wealthy, but is the kind of man who makes one think of Wendell Phillips' remark, that "the Lord showed his estimate of money by the people he gave it to." Why should you be jealous of such rivals? You stand at least as good a chance as they.

Fred. No I don't. Look here, I've just been made a member of the firm. That will give me something like $4,000 a year at first. How can I ask a girl living as she does to try and get along on that?

Stuart. You forget her own income.

Fred. That's just what I can't do. I've tried to tell her that I love her, but her money makes the words stick in my throat.

Stuart. And yet Van Tromp, who hasn't a cent in the world, and never will have, if he has to make it himself, will say it as glibly as need be.

Fred. It's that makes me desperate. I try to be good company, but I feel all the time as if it were n't an even race, and so I can't.

Stuart. My dear boy, no race in this world is even. If it were anything but a woman's heart in question, I would bet on you as the winner; but as that commodity is only to be represented by the algebraic *x*, I never wager on it.

Fred (scornfully). How learnedly a bachelor does talk of women's hearts! One would think he had broken a lot in order to examine their contents.

Stuart (a little angrily). I never lost a girl through faint heart, — or lost my temper with both her and my best friend.

Fred (apologetically). There! Of course you are right and I am a fool.

Stuart (looking at watch). There being no dissent to that opinion, and the ladies being now ready to see us, you had better go downstairs and show Miss Wortley that the Fred Stevens of a year ago is still in the flesh.

Fred (going to b. d.). And you?

Stuart. I 'll stay here and have a cigar.

[*Exit* FRED, *b. d.*

Stuart (taking out cigar-case). How that

poor fellow does carry his heart in view!
(*Takes match from desk.*)   No wonder
Miss Wortley keeps hers to herself, with
such an example !   [*Strikes match.*

Enter POLLY, *l. d., carrying black domino
and lace mask.*

Stuart.   Hello !   One minute, please.
Whose domino is that ?

Polly (*halting*).   I must n't tell, sir.

Stuart.   No, of course not.   Quite
right.   (*Tosses away match and jingles coins
in his pocket.*)   Perhaps, though, you can
tell me to whom you are carrying it.

Polly (*coming down*).   Perhaps I might,
sir.

Stuart (*taking out money*).   Well ?

Polly.   I was carrying it to Mrs. Van
Tromp's room, sir.

Stuart (*giving money*).   Thank you.
(*Takes domino and mask from her.*)   Mr.
Stuart told you Miss Wortley wanted you to
come at once to her, and so you left these
in this room — understand ?   (*Gives more
money.*)   Now be off to your mistress.

Polly. Yes, sir.   [*Exit* POLLY *l. d.*

Stuart. It's better to be born lucky than rich. (*Pats domino tenderly, and arranges it neatly in chair c.*) You're luckier, though, for you belong to the dearest and most heartless woman in this world. (*Looks at mask.*) And you! She doesn't need you to mask her feelings, confound and bless her inscrutable face! You'll be pressing against it ere long. (*Kisses mask.*) Take that to her.

Mrs. V. T. (outside). No, I sent Polly for my domino, but she hasn't brought it.

Stuart. Speaking of angels — And she mustn't discover that I know.

> [*Hurriedly seizes mask and domino and tosses them behind curtains of bay window; then strikes match as if about to light cigar.*

MRS. VAN TROMP *appears at b. d. and looks in.*

Mrs. V. T. Shall it be a cigar or my society? "Under which king, Bezonian? Speak or die."

Stuart (*throwing match in fire*). That goes without saying. The cigar is my slave; I am Mrs. Van Tromp's!

Mrs. V. T. Was that impromptu?

Stuart. Coined for the occasion, and needing only the approval of your majesty to make it gold in my eyes. [*Bows.*

Mrs. V. T. I am too good a queen to help stamp worthless money, and that 's what a compliment is. As the French say, " Fine words cost nothing and are worth just what they cost."

Stuart. Anglisé in " Fine words butter no parsnips." You know, I 've always wanted to send that proverb to Delmonico. He takes something uneatable, and by giving it a sauce and a high-sounding French title, deludes the public into ordering it. You pay five cents for the basis, ten for the sauce, and the other thirty-five for the French, which no man can understand or pronounce.

Mrs. V. T. He did n't serve this evening's dinner.

Stuart. Far be it from me to suggest

that there was anything wrong in the cuisine to-night. The only criticism I could possibly make on the dinner was that there were twenty-four too many people.

Mrs. V. T. (*counting on fingers*). Twenty-four from twenty-six — that leaves two?

Stuart. Let me congratulate you on your mental arithmetic.

Mrs. V. T. Have you actually reached that time of life when one ceases to enjoy dinners?

Stuart. I hope not. I was even flattering myself that my tastes were becoming more juvenile.

Mrs. V. T. In what does that show itself?

Stuart. In wanting something I can't have. I believe it's considered infantile to want the moon.

Mrs. V. T. You want the moon? Then you must be in love! I'm so sorry I can't stay and let you tell me all about her. I came upstairs for my domino and must n't tarry.   [*Starts up back.*

Stuart (*standing between her and the door*). One moment, Mrs. Van Tromp. I'll not bore you with my own love affair, but I should like to ask your help in another.

Mrs. V. T. (*turning and coming down l.*). I promise my assistance. I love to help on — other people's love affairs.

Stuart. There is a poor fellow downstairs who is eating his heart out with love for your cousin Agnes. He thinks you are against him.

Mrs. V. T. You mean Mr. Stevens?

Stuart. Yes.

Mrs. V. T. Why, Mr. Stuart, I like Mr. Stevens, and he would be my second choice —

Stuart (*interrupting*). For yourself?

Mrs. V. T. (*laughing*). No, for Agnes. But surely you don't expect me to work against my brother-in-law?

Stuart. But Agnes is your cousin. Do consider her!

Mrs. V. T. Mr. Stuart, I married Alexander Van Tromp without caring that (*snaps her fingers*) for him. Yet we hit it off together very nicely. He obtained income and I won social position. By it I have been able to introduce my uncle into good society, and give Agnes her pick of the best. Do you think I do her wrong in planning the same kind of a marriage for her?

Stuart. Has Cupid no rights?

Mrs. V. T. He can come later. The Van Tromps are too old a family for the members to live long. So I am only giving Agnes a few years of matrimony, like my own; and then — well, you know whether my life is gloomy or otherwise.

Stuart. Mostly otherwise, I should say.

Mrs. V. T. No girl of nineteen knows enough to pick out the man she can breakfast with three hundred and sixty-five days in the year for half a century. Moreover, a young girl cannot have a large enough choice. She can only say " yes " or " no " to those who ask her. On the contrary, a woman of — we 'll say twenty-eight — picks out her man and fascinates him. To quote the French again : " A girl of sixteen accepts love; a woman of thirty incites it."

Stuart. As you have been doing?

Mrs. V. T. Agnes shall sample matrimony with Regie; see just what it is like; and then be prepared to select a second time with wisdom and discrimination — like her aged and venerable cousin.

Stuart (*hesitatingly*). Will you pardon the question, —but was Mr. — was, ah, the brother of Reginald anything like, ah, his brother?

Mrs. V. T. (*laughing*). Very!

Stuart (*confidentially*). What did you do with him?

Mrs. V. T. On the day we married, he put a ring on my finger; I put one through his nose. Then he led very nicely.

Stuart. And is that your ideal of a husband?

Mrs. V. T. Unless I find a man capable of not merely doing the leading, but by whom I shall wish to be led.

Stuart. And how is this man to prove his capacity?

Mrs. V. T. Oh, it's merely a matter of cleverness or mastery. Let a man out-wit me, and I will (*curtseys*) ever after sign myself, "Your obedient, humble servant."

Stuart. Don't you see that you are bribing your own undoing?

Mrs. V. T. How so?

Stuart. Why, your conditions are al-most in the nature of a challenge. Now you know, of course, Mrs. Van Tromp, that I don't love you, yet you make me want to enter the rather formidable com-petition just to see if I could n't get the better of you.

Mrs. V. T. (*laughing*). Well, I have no wish to balk you. But it must be a game of forfeits. If you fail, you must pay a penalty.

Stuart. Is n't failure to win Mrs. Van Tromp penalty enough?

Mrs. V. T. Not to so confirmed a bachelor as Mr. Stuart. Come, if you beat me, I will do any one thing you wish ; if you are beaten, you must do the one thing I wish. Is it a bargain ?

Stuart. Done! (*Kissing Mrs. V. T.'s hand.*) Perdition have my soul !

Mrs. V. T. And now for my domino.

[*Hurries up and exits l. d.*

Stuart (*at l. d.*). But, Mrs. Van Tromp, you have n't told me in what I am to beat you ? [*Exit* STUART, *l. d.*

Enter CHARLIE *and* AGNES, *b. d.*

Charlie. Thith ith better than down thairth, Mith Wortley, ith n't it?

Agnes (*sinking into chair c. with sigh*). Oh, much !

Charlie. I 've been wanting to thuggeth it before, Mith Wortley, but that bore Van Tromp wath alwayth round, and if he heard me, he would intrude hith thothiety upon uth.

Agnes. Why, Mr. Newbank, I thought you were friends.

Charlie. We uthed to be, till the fellowth came out thuth a thnob.

Agnes. That is where you men have such an advantage. Now we girls have to put up with every donkey that comes near us.

Charlie. That ith hard, Mith Wortley. But it theemth to me that you might thave yourthelf by a little diplomathy.

Agnes (*eagerly*). Do tell me how!

Charlie. Why don't you get rid of Van Tromp?

Agnes. Why, I can't be rude to him. You must remember he is a relation.

Charlie. I did n't mean rudneth.

Agnes. What then?

Charlie Why, he athkth you to danth; you are out of breath or tired. He thitth down by you; you want a glath of lemonade, or thomething elth, it doth n't matter what.

Agnes (*aside*). Does he really think that 's an original idea? (*Aloud.*) How clever!

Charlie. Yeth, I rather think thatth a good nothon.

Agnes. Is n't it warm here?

Charlie. Very. I've thought of thug-gethting that we open a window.

Agnes. Oh, I'm so afraid of drafts. Did you see where I left my fan?

Charlie. No, — unleth you left it down thairth in the library.

Agnes. Won't you see if I did?

Charlie (going up l. b.). With the greateth of pleathure.

Agnes. And, Mr. Newbank, (*Charlie turns*) don't tell Mr. Van Tromp I'm here.   [REG. *appears at b. d.*

Charlie. I'll tell any lie thooner. (*Turns.*) Ah!! (*Politely.*) Mither Van Tromp, Mith Wortley ith fatigued and wanth to retht a little.

Reg. Aw! Then she shows gweat good sense in sending you away.

Charlie (angrily). Thir, you thould n't inflict your thothiety on a lady who hath juth been athking me how to get rid of you.

Reg. (coolly). I hope you told her it was by keeping you about her.

Charlie. If thatth the cathe, I'll be back very thoon.   [*Exits b. d.*

Reg. Aw, I 'm deucid sowy that boah Newbank has tired you, Miss Wortley. You weally should not be so awfully good natured, don't cher know.

Agnes. Oh, we have to be, and he 's no worse than a lot of others.

Reg. I jolly wish, you know, that I could save you fwom it.

Agnes. Don't you think it warm here?

Reg. Weally, but it is, pon honour.

Agnes. And I 'm so thirsty. Would it trouble you too much to get me a glass of water?

Reg. (rising and going up l.). Chawmed, I assure you.

CHARLIE *appears b. d. and they run into each other.*

Reg. Aw, I thought you were going to allow Miss Wortley a little west.

Charlie. Thatth why I wath coming back. I did n't think the would thend you away.

Reg. I 'll be back soon, deah boy.

[*Exits b. d.*

Charlie. I'm thorry, Mith Wortley, but your fan ith not in the library.

Agnes (*aside*). Tell me something I don't know. (*Aloud.*) Have the rest of the men finished their cigars?

Charlie. Yeth.

Agnes. I suppose I ought to go down.

[*Rises.*

Charlie. Yeth, we'll go together, and tho ethcape Van Tromp.

Agnes (*aside*). What a pity some glue company can't buy those two and melt them down into mucilage! (*Aloud.*) Yes, but first won't you see if I did n't leave my fan on the piano in the music-room?

Charlie. Why, thertainly.

[*Starts up to b. d.*

Agnes (*aside*). While you're gone I'll get into my domino, and if you catch me afterwards, it's my fault.

[*Exit* CHARLIE. *Loud exclamation outside.*

Charlie (*outside*). You donkey, you ran into me on purpoth, and thpilled that water on me.

Agnes.   Do for once temper the wind to the shorn lamb !

> [*Looks around room helplessly, and then rushes to bay window and hides.*

Reg. (*outside*).   I beg pawdon, but it was you who wan into me.   Cawnt cher see where you are going?

REG. *appears b. d. with a glass containing very little water, wiping his coat sleeve with handkerchief, and looking angrily after* CHARLIE.

Reg.   I'm deucid sowy, Miss Wortley, but that clumsy fool has spilled most of the water (*coming down*).   One can always tell the *nouveaux* wiche by their gaucherwies. (*Finds chair empty —starts, and looks round room.*) Pon honour, if he hasn't dwiven her away !   [*Stands looking about.*

CHARLIE *appears at b. d.*

Charlie.   I met your maid, Mith Wortley, and the thaid your fan wath in your room, (*coming down r.*) and that the'll get it. (*Discovers Agnes' absence.*)   Now then,

I hope you are thatithfied with having driven her away.

Reg.   Oh, I dwove her away, did I?

Charlie.   Yeth.

Reg. (*laughing*).   That is wich!

Charlie.   Well, thath more than you are!

Reg.   Cholly Newbank, you get worse form everwy day.

Enter POLLY *with fan l. d.*

Polly.   Here is the fan, Mr. Newbank.

Charlie (*taking fan*).   Can you tell me where Mith Wortley ith?

Polly (*starting to go*).   No, sir.

STUART *appears in b. d. and stands and listens.*

Charlie.   One moment, girl.   (*To Reg.*) Mither Van Tromp, will you oblige me by leaving the room?

Reg.   By Jove!   The bwass of the man would start a foundwy.

[*Sits chair l. with emphasis.*

Charlie.   Thir, in the future I thall refuth to recognith you.

Reg. Thanks, awfully.

Charlie (*taking bank-note from pocket*). Girl, do you thee thith?

Polly. Oh, yes, sir.

Charlie. What ith Mith Wortleyth domino like?

Polly. Oh, indeed, sir, I don't dare to tell you.

Charlie. Nonthenth! The 'll never know who told. You might ath well make five dollarth.

Polly. But Mr. Van Tromp might tell.

Reg. (*with extreme dignity*). Mr. Van Tromp is too much of a gentleman to either bwibe or tell tales.

Charlie. But he 'll lithen all the thame!

Polly (*fearfully*). She's going to wear a white silk one with cardinal ribbons, and a black lace veil.

[*Receives note and exits l.*

Charlie (*triumphantly*). Ah! Now I have her.

Reg. Deucid sowy to spoil your little dweam, but I fahncy I shall speak to her myself this evening.

Charlie (gleefully). All right. The knowth you are after her money.

Stuart (coming down). Ah ! Damon and Pythias together as usual. It really gives one faith in friendship to see how you two fellows run together.

Charlie. Mither Thuart, did you ever hear anything more nonthenthical than for Van Tromp to thuppothe that Mith Wortley ith going to thave him from the poorhouth ?

Reg. (with dignity). Mr. Stuart will tell you that a born gentleman can do much that is impossible to the canaille.

Charlie (angrily). What do you mean by that, thir?

Reg. Pway dwaw your own conclusions.

Stuart (sitting on desk). And so you two bloods intend to question the oracle ? I had n't credited you with the courage.

Charlie. It doth n't need much when one knowth what the anther will be.

Reg. (confidently). I 'm not afwaid for my part, but even " no " would n't make me commit suicide.

Charlie.   Thath prethuth fortunate for you, but hard on the reth of uth.

Stuart (*quizzically*).   Oh, it's easy enough to propose to a girl when she is n't present.   You fellows forget that Miss Wortley is a masked battery this evening.   It takes pluck to face one of them, and I don't believe you 'll either of you dare do it.

Charlie.   I 'd like to bet a monkey I will.

Stuart.   Done!   And do the same with you, Van Tromp.

Charlie.   He hath n't the money.

Reg. (*glancing scornfully at Charlie*). You 'll oblige me gweatly by minding your own affairs.   Done, Mr. Stuart.

Enter FRED *b. d.*

Stuart.   Ah, Fred, you 've just missed a rare bit of sport.

Fred.   What was that ?

Stuart.   Why, we 've just wagered —

Reg. (*dignified*).   I beg pawdon, Mr. Stuart, but I had always supposed a wager was a confidential mattah.

[*Walks with dignity up r. and exits
b. d.*

Charlie. For onth in hith life, Van
Tromp ith right.

[*Bows grandly and goes up l.
Exits b. d.*

Stuart (*laughing*). I thought that would
get rid of them. Well, have you shown
Miss Wortley that you can still be occasionally jolly?

Fred (*gloomily*). I have n't had the
chance. She must be in her room, for
I 've looked everywhere else for her. Not
that it 's much loss. I know I should not
have been in the mood to please her.

Stuart. That 's because you don't try
hard enough.

Fred (*bitterly*). Hear the bachelor
talk of making love!

Stuart. You think me ignorant?

Fred. Rather, — judging from the re-
sults.

Stuart (*resting hand on Fred's shoulder*).
Fred, I 'm not the kind of a man who
lets the world know what he 's thinking

about. With all due respect to a young fellow who is not far distant, it does n't pay to show one's feelings too much. But I 'm going to tell you my bit of romance as an object-lesson. Two months ago I met the most charming woman in the world, and could no more help falling in love —

Fred (*looking up in surprise*). What! The ideal bachelor in love?

Stuart. I don't see why two and forty should be debarred from that universal sensation, any more than four and twenty.

Fred. Oh, of course not, — only, to make an Irish bull, we had all grown to think you as wedded to celibacy.

Stuart. There are divorces and desertions in celibacy as well as in matrimony. Well, I love this woman; I don't think she loves me, — though you never can tell with a clever one, and sometimes I think she is beginning to like me, because she — because she tries to make me believe she is worse than she is. She delights in making me think she 's a devil, which shows that she is a bit afraid of me. I've never said a word of my love to her, but she knows it as well as I do. But nobody else dreams of it. I don't make my attentions so obvious that every one sees them, and so cause her embarrassment whenever I even come into the room. I don't cut up rough if she talks or dances with other fellows. I simply try to be pleasant and useful enough to make her prefer my society to that of any other man.

Fred (*sighing*). Well, of course you are right, but — tell me what you think I ought to do.

Stuart (*walking to desk and holding bell*). What do you suppose would happen if I rang this? [*Rings.*

Fred. That does n't answer my question.

Stuart. I want to see if the bell won't save me the trouble.

Enter POLLY, *l. d.*

Polly. Did you ring, sir?

Stuart. Yes, I want to find out if you

told the truth about Miss Wortley's domino?

Polly (*embarrassed*). Well, sir, Miss Wortley has two dominos, and I don't know which she intends to wear first.

Stuart. What is the other domino like?

Polly. It's blue with silver lace.

Stuart. What will you charge me to wear the white and cardinal one this evening, leaving Miss Wortley only the blue and silver one?

Polly (*eagerly*). Oh, Mr. Stuart, that's just what I've wanted to do, but have n't dared! Please don't tempt me.

Stuart. Fudge! If you'll do as I'll tell you, you shall have a year's wages to-morrow.

Polly. Gracious!!

Stuart. Is it a bargain?

Polly (*eagerly*). Yes, sir. What am I to do?

Stuart. H'm. Can you write a good hand?

Polly. Ask Mr. Stevens?

Stuart (reproachfully). Oh, Fred !!

Fred. I don't know what she means.

Polly. I wrote that note to-day thanking you for the flowers : I write nearly all Miss Wortley's notes.

Fred. Bosh !

> [*During letter-writing he surreptitiously dives into inside pocket and produces glove, handkerchief, faded flowers, and letters tied with ribbon. Examines letters, and then crosses to mantel, tears them up, and throws them into fire.*

Stuart. Good ! It could n't be better. They 'll think it 's Miss Wortley's handwriting. Sit down at that desk and write as I dictate.

Polly. Yes, sir.

> [*Sits at desk — business of letter-writing.*

Stuart. " My own : Driven to the verge of desperation by the parasites who cluster about my wealth, I long for nothing but a refuge. This you can give me, and if you cherish one emotion of tenderness for me, you will be in the little morning room at twelve. A." Address that to Newbank. Now take another sheet. "Reginald: If you have one spark of affection for me, keep me no longer in suspense! I shall be in the little morning room over the supper-room at ten minutes after twelve. Fly then to your loving but unhappy A." Address that to Van Tromp. Now, Polly, you must deliver those notes in person, get into Miss Wortley's domino, and be here at that time. Newbank will propose to you, and you must accept him and get rid of him. Then you must do the same to Van Tromp. Understand?

Polly. Yes, Mr. Stuart.

[*Rises with two notes in hand.*

Stuart. And you must n't let them find out their mistake till to-morrow.

[*Exits* POLLY *b. d.*

Fred. Do you think that 's honourable?

Stuart. It 's too soon after dinner for me to discuss ethics. But for you it 's the chance of a lifetime. You know what Miss Wortley is to wear. Go and make yourself agreeable to her, and if her mask gives you courage, tell her that you love her.

Fred. You don't understand. I'm not afraid to tell her that to her face. It's not the woman I'm afraid of. If she were poor, I could have said to her as I say to myself, fifty times a day, " I love you." But I can't say that to her money.

Stuart. And so you are going to place your Brunhilde on the top of her gold and then fear to climb the fiery mountain? Why, Fred, tell her that you love her, and leave it for her to decide whether it's the woman or the wealth you care for.

Fred. I can't bear to give her the chance even to think I'm sordid.

Stuart. Nonsense, my boy! Go and tell Miss Wortley that you love her before it's too late. Make her the prettiest compliment a man can pay a woman, and if she has the bad taste to think it's her money and not her beauty and sweetness, you are no worse off.

Fred. Mr. Stuart, I've tried to say it and to write it. I've begun sentence after sentence; I've torn up letter after letter. It's no good.

Stuart (wearily). I don't see anything to be done, except to get your proposal made by proxy. (*Stops short in walk.*) By Jove, that's an idea.

Fred. What?

Stuart (triumphantly). I have it. I'll get into a domino, pass myself off for you, and propose. [*Goes up back.*

Fred (angrily). You'll do nothing of the kind!

Stuart. Why not?

Fred. Mr. Stuart, your proposition is simply insulting. A moment since you said that a declaration of love was the greatest compliment a man could pay a woman, and now you would turn it into a joke or trick. Do you think I will allow the woman I love to be so treated?

Stuart (soothingly). All right. We'll say no more about it. [*At b. d.*

Fred. Then give me your word you won't.

Stuart. That's another matter.

Fred. Then I shall at once find Miss Wortley and —

Stuart (interrupting). Tell her all about it. That's right. You will have told her that you love her. [*Exits b. d.*

Fred (following). Not at all! I shall simply keep near her, and if you make the attempt I shall interfere. [*Exits b. d.*

[AGNES *rises from concealment, peeks out and comes down c, with* MRS. V. T.'s *domino and mask on her arm.*

Agnes. At last! I began to think I should have to spend the night there, — though I did nearly burst in on them two or three times. And that's the way men discuss women! (*Scornfully.*) So, Mr. Van Tromp, I'm to save you from the poorhouse! And "no" would n't make you commit suicide! And you're not afraid of what my answer will be, Mr. Newbank! Oh!!! (*Laughs.*) I should like to hear their proposals to Polly. I 've always thought that girl a treasure, but she gets her dismissal to-morrow. The idea of wearing my domino, and telling all those men what I was to wear! And telling Mr. Stevens that she wrote my letters for me! (*Anxiously.*) What must he think of me! And the only one of them too who seemed to think I deserve the commonest courtesy. " I could say to Miss Wortley, as I say to myself fifty times a day, I love you." (*Demurely.*) That was nice! I wonder if he — I wonder if Mr. Stuart will propose to me? I never thought he would behave so badly. (*Pacing across stage meditatively.*) How can I turn the tables and punish them all? Let me see — (*checking off on fingers*) — the two puppies will be punished by the loss of their bets and — me! Polly will lose her position. Now —

Enter Mrs. V. T. *l. d.*

Mrs. V. T. Oh, Agnes, I can't find my domino anywhere, and — Why, you have it!

Agnes (as if seized with an inspiration).
Frances, you must let me change dominos
and masks with you.

Mrs. V. T. What for?

Agnes. Mr. Stuart has bribed Polly to
tell about our dominos, — and he's going
to propose to my blue one.

Mrs. V. T. (incredulously). What, — to
you?

Agnes (embarrassed). Oh! That is —
Well — he's — You see it's — he's only
asking for some one else."

Mrs. V. T. Oh, I see! Some one
who hasn't dared?

Agnes. Yes. Mr. Newbank is so —

Mrs. V. T. Of course. He is shy.

Agnes. Very. *(Hurriedly.)* And so I
thought we could change dominos, and —
and — don't you see?

Mrs. V. T. (reflectively). But then —
Wouldn't — Oh! Why, of course I will.
Here, let me help you on with it; and now
run along downstairs. The dancing is in
full swing.

Agnes (going up). I'll go at once.

(*Turns in b. d.*)   You will find my domino
in my dressing-room.   [*Exits l. d.*

Mrs. V. T. (*reflectively*).   And so Mr.
Stuart is going to propose to a blue
domino — that's me — on behalf of Mr.
Stevens? (*Laughs.*)   There's a nice game
of cross purposes.   Ah, sir, you'll have
to be cleverer than that to —   What a
chance to beat him!   Let me see.

STUART *appears at b. d.*

Stuart.   Not masked yet?
Mrs. V. T.   Ah! Mr. Stuart, I am
ready to name our game of forfeits.
Stuart (*coming down*).   Bravo!
Mrs. V. T.   You want to win my
cousin for Mr. Stevens.   Succeed, and you
shall name whatever forfeit you choose.
Fail, and I set what penalty I please.
Stuart.   Agreed.
Mrs. V. T.   But I warn you: I shall
stoop to anything rather than be beaten.
If a man is honourable he will be at a
great disadvantage.   Like Faust, I have
made a pact with the devil.

Stuart. Better take a partner with whom I am on less friendly relations.

Mrs. V. T. He is not on so good terms with you as with me. Don't you know that women are extremes? That they are either a great deal better or worse than men?

Stuart. I have always heard that women said spiteful things of their sex, but I don't think it's nice of you to make such speeches about the one I care for. One would almost think you were jealous of her.

Mrs. V. T. (*throwing glove on floor*). There is my challenge to the combat.

Stuart (*picking it up*). I accept the gage.

Mrs. V. T. (*holding out hand*). But not to keep it.

Stuart. I will only return the glove without the *g*.

Mrs. V. T. And without that letter, I prefer to get a new pair. [*Going up.*

Stuart (*following*). Then it is real war?

Mrs. V. T. War, fierce and merciless.

[*Exit* Mrs. V. T. *and* Stuart, *b. d.*

POLLY *peeks in l. d., then enters with white domino and mask on arm.*

Polly. I did n't dare to put this on (*putting on domino and mask*) in Miss Wortley's room for fear she might come in. What will she say when she only finds one? My! I shall have to keep out of her way this evening, or she will want to know who is wearing it. (*Looking down at domino.*) Oh, I wish I dared go to Miss Wortley's dressing-room and look at myself in the glass! (*Walks off, looking behind her.*) I will. (*Goes up to l. d. and starts to exit.*) Oh, Jiminy!

[*Turns and rushes out b. d.*

Enter AGNES *l. d. in domino, and with mask in her hand.*

Agnes (*coming down*). I changed my mind about going downstairs, for I had rather miss all the dancing in the world than puppydom's love-making to the back-stairs. I could almost forgive Polly when I think of what I have in store. (*Crosses r. and looks through curtains at bay window.*) From my hiding-place, I'll hear every word of it. (*Goes to mantel and looks at clock.*) Quarter to twelve — I'm early!

STUART *appears at b. d. and looks in.*

Agnes. Ah! [*Hurriedly masks herself.*
Stuart (*aside*). That's the quickest change I ever saw. I only just left her at the door of her room! (*Comes down.*) Are you practising lightning transformations?
Agnes. Comment ça va-t-il, Monsieur?
Stuart (*regretfully*). I'm sorry, but I don't understand French. (*Aside.*) Whopper number one.
Agnes. Wie gehts?
Stuart. Nor German. (*Aside.*) Number two.
Agnes. Buenas noches, señor?
Stuart (*wearily*). And on Spanish I'm an entire failure. (*Aside.*) The recording angel did n't catch me that time!
Agnes. Will you kindly tell me what you do speak?

Stuart (*gallantly and bowing*). In your society only the universal language.

Agnes. And I don't understand Volapük.

Stuart. Volapük! That's not the one of which I speak.

Agnes. And of what, then?

Stuart. To the language which without instruction is known around the world; to the language that's spoken by all classes, and is never out of fashion; to the language that has no dictionary; yet which possesses the most beautiful vocabulary in the universe.

Agnes. I don't remember any such in my text-book on philology.

Stuart. It is too real to be taught in schools. Nor were you old enough to understand it had it been. I speak of the language of love.

Agnes. Of course; I suppose it is a universal tongue. (*Satirically.*) But so few can speak it well. Don't you think it ought to be left to the poets?

Stuart. I love the future of the human race too much to wish that. Think of the frightful increase of bad rhymers it would cause, — and that too with the markets already overstocked.

Agnes. But would that be any worse than to see the average unromantic bread-winner make love? It's very hard on our sex to appear sympathetic. Most men do it about as successfully as a hippopotamus would waltz.

Stuart. Are n't you a little unfair, Mrs. Van Tromp?

Agnes. And so you think I am Mrs. Van Tromp?

Stuart. I don't think it; I know it. Do you think for a moment you could deceive me? But that does n't answer my question.

Agnes. As to the justice of my criticism on the way men propose? (*With affected coyness.*) Perhaps I have had too little experience to speak with knowledge.

Stuart. Mrs. Van Tromp would not dare to say that unmasked. Her face would give her tongue the lie.

Agnes. I fancy you are the first man who ever turned calling one a liar into a compliment.

Stuart.   Since that is possible, may not a poetic proposal be also ?

Agnes.   Perhaps.   And when I hear one that does not make me want to laugh, I 'll make public recantation.

Stuart.   It 's a bold man or a fool who 'd venture after what you have said.   And yet I should like to try.

Agnes (laughing).   Why, Mr. Stuart, what would you do if I were to take you seriously and say yes ?

Stuart (with mock resignation).   Bear it — like a man.   But I am quite safe from that danger !   I trust you won't mind if in the passion of the moment I call you Frances.

Agnes.   This once I 'll condone the liberty.

Stuart (coming very close to Agnes). And if I should so far forget myself as to try and — well, behave as lovers generally do ?

Agnes (retreating).   Oh, Mrs. Van Tromp is quite safe from that.

[*Slips past* STUART *and crosses to l.*

Stuart (aside). Don't be too sure of that.

Agnes. Well, begin.

Stuart (crossing to chair c.). Now that's no way to give a lover an opening. I want this to have verisimilitude. In real life you don't as good as say to the man (*sits very much on the edge of chair c.*) sitting on the edge of his chair, ' Please begin.' Do let's make it realistic.

Agnes (laughing). Even to the mitten ? Very well. (*Imitating society manner.*) I did n't see you at Mrs. Grainger's rose-cotillion Tuesday, Mr. Stuart.

Charlie (without). Ah ! My angel, we meet.

Agnes (seizing Stuart's hand). Quick ! Come !

[*Drags him over to bay window, where she conceals both with curtain.*

Enter POLLY, *in mask and domino, and* CHARLIE *b. d.*

Charlie. My own ! What can I do to thow my gratitude ?

Polly. If you but knew how I have trembled at my unmaidenly imprudence in writing you !

Charlie. My angel, love knowth no prudenth ; no boundth can limit it.

Polly. And you don't scorn and despise me ?

Charlie. Thcorn ? Dethpithe ? Never.

Polly. And you don't think me unmaidenly ?

Charlie. It ith impothible. You are nothing but what ith perfect and beautiful.

Polly (*sighing*).   Ah !

Charlie (*sighing*).   Ah !   (*Reaches out and takes her hand.*)   Mith Wortley, did you mean what you thaid in your letter ?

Polly (*languishing*).   Can you doubt it ?

Charlie. And you really love your Cholly ?

Polly (*tenderly*).   Oh, Cholly !

Charlie (*kneeling*).   And you really want to marry your Cholly ?

Polly (*faintly*).   Oh, Cholly !

Reginald *appears b. d. and enters.*

Reg. Miss Wortley, I have hurwied to your side. And none too soon, it appears.

Charlie (*jumping to his feet and speaking very angrily*). You thpethimen of the horroth of heredity, you get out of here!

Polly (*sotto voce to Charlie*). Oh, please don't make a disturbance! Remember whose house it is! Leave us and I'll get rid of him and follow.

Charlie. My angel, I can refuth you nothing. (*Goes up stage and speaks to Reg.*) Thir, you owe your thafety to that lady. [*Exit b. d.*

Reg. (*coming down*). Miss Wortley, I am deucid sowy that epitome of bad form has been borwing you.

Polly. Oh, I don't mind that. I was only afraid he was going to misbehave.

Reg. Aw, the cad's always doing that, don'tcher know.

Polly. Oh, Mr. Van Tromp, what must you think of me!

Reg. Think of you? The woman Reginald De Lancey Van Tromp loves is above thought. In but one way can the loveliest of her sex offend me.

Polly (eagerly). Ah! Tell me, so that I may never do it.

Reg. By wefusing the heart and hand he (*kneeling*) places at her feet.

Polly. Oh! I am faint with too great happiness. (*Leans on Reg.*) Reginald, support — Oh, Jiminy! Some one's coming.

  [*Recovers, and rushes up l. to l. b.,
   exit l. d. followed by* REG.

Enter MRS. VAN TROMP *and* FRED, *b. d.*

Mrs. V. T. (*coming down*). I told you we should find this room empty.

       [*Looks about.*

Fred. But that does n't tell me why you asked me to bring you here.

Mrs. V. T. Perhaps to cheat you out of your dance with our host's pretty daughter.

Fred. I might answer you in kind. But it 's fairer to tell you that your mask is no disguise.

Mrs. V. T. You know me?

Fred. Yes. You are "our host's pretty daughter."

Mrs. V. T. I am but a poor actress if I have played my part so badly.

Fred. Indeed, no. Even now I find it hard to believe, your acting is so perfect. If I had not known your domino, I should never have recognised you.

Mrs. V. T. My domino?

Fred. I overheard it mentioned. I was sorry to learn your secret, but really I could n't help it.

Mrs. V. T. It really does not matter. But I am glad you told me. Most men would have kept mum and let me talk on about "our host's pretty daughter," and then have never let me hear the last of it.

Fred. I 'm afraid I 'm no better than the rest of my sex, Miss Wortley. With most women I should have done that.

Mrs. V. T. And why am I an exception?

Fred. I did n't want to deceive you.

Mrs. V. T. Why not?

Fred. Because I wanted you to think well of me.

Mrs. V. T. Why, I do that already. If you only knew how I respected and admired the men who have been real friends, and not seekers of my money!

Fred. Miss Wortley, I thank you for your kind thoughts of me, but you must n't think them any longer.

Mrs. V. T. Why not?

Fred. Because I don't deserve them. Do you remember our first meeting?

Mrs. V. T. (aside). Gracious! I hope I 'm not to be cross-examined. (*Aloud, hesitatingly.*) It was on a yacht, was n't it?

Fred. After that cruise I came back to my desk and bachelor quarters, but neither they nor I have been the same since. It 's always seemed to me as if a bit of heaven had come into my life in those days. Every hour since has been consecrated to an ideal. I have worked as I was never able to work before. And why? Because I was straining every fibre to win money and position enough to be able to come to you and say : " Miss Wortley, I love you as a man must love one so sweet and beautiful. I 'm not rich, but if you can care for me enough to make a few sacrifices I will try and keep you from regretting them, by love and tenderness.

Mrs. V. T. But, Mr. Stevens, you seem to forget that the man I marry will be made rich at once. (*Aside.*) Ugh, I feel like a brute.

Fred. I 've tried to forget it, but I could n't. It has come between us in the past ; is it to do so in the future ?

Mrs. V. T. Mr. Stevens, I can't tell you my grief in finding you like the rest of my disinterested masculine friends.

Fred (*hotly*). You think I care for your money ?

Mrs. V. T. What else can I think ? (*Aside.*) You cat !

Agnes (*starting to pull aside curtain, sotto voce to Stuart*). Oh ! I must n't —

Stuart (*checking her*). No, don't interfere, Mrs. Van Tromp. Let the poor fellow take the whole dose while he's about it.

Fred (*who has gone up back and now comes down*). Miss Wortley, do you realize what you are saying? In the last minute you have three times deliberately insulted me. Say you don't love me, if that is so, but don't impute shameful motives to my love. It is of value to me if worthless to you.

Mrs. V. T. Mr. Stevens, frankness under such circumstances is best for all. Put yourself in my place. I am an heiress, with expectations from my father. You acknowledge yourself that you are poor. Don't blame me if I draw my own conclusions.

Fred. But I will blame you, and it is the last time I shall ever trouble you. You ask me to put myself in your place: let us try the reverse. I offer you a love as true and unmercenary as was ever offered a woman. What do I deserve at your hands? Mercy, at least. But instead, you — you have not been content to reject it — you have poisoned it forever.

> [*Turns and walks up stage to b. d.* MRS. VAN TROMP *begins to take off mask.* AGNES *springs from bay window, and rushes forward c.*

Agnes. One moment, Mr. Stevens. (*To Mrs. V. T. tearfully.*) Oh, Frances, how could you ?

Mrs. V. T. (*taking off mask*). I couldn't. I was unmasking to show him his mistake.

> [FRED *stands hesitating, looking from one to the other.* STUART'S *head through curtains.*

Fred. You are not Miss Wortley ?

Agnes (*taking off mask*). No, Mr. Stevens. Miss Wortley never thought you a fortune-hunter. She remembers perfectly the first time she met you. She's glad she brought a little heaven into your life. She's glad that you — that you —

Fred (rushing down stage). That I love you ?

Agnes. Yes.

Fred. And you are willing to make the sacrifice ?

Agnes. Yes.

Fred. And you care for me ?

Agnes. No (*holds out her hand*), I love you.

Fred (taking and kissing it). My treasure !　　　　[*Both retire up back l.*

Mrs. V. T. Heigho ! That 's what comes of wrong-doing. In trying to win my wager, I 've actually helped Mr. Stuart to beat me.

Stuart (head through curtains). For which I can't thank you enough !

Mrs. V. T. You !

Stuart. Exactly ! Are n't you ashamed ?
　　　　　　　　　　[*Comes out c.*

Mrs. V. T. Of being defeated ? Yes. But don't be too triumphant. You did n't win single-handed.

Stuart. I certainly did not have much assistance, except from Mrs. Van Tromp.

Mrs. V. T. On the contrary, you had the best assistance in the world. I ought to have known better than bet against so powerful a coalition as Mr. Stuart and Cupid. I only hope my behaviour has made me odious to you!

[*Crosses petulantly to r.*

Stuart. On the contrary, I'm rather fond of real deviltry! So, if agreeable, we'll settle the stakes at once.

Mrs. V. T. I throw myself on your mercy.

Stuart. And what mercy would you have shown me, had I lost?

Mrs. V. T. Yes, but then I'm a woman.

Stuart. Deo gratia.

Mrs. V. T. And you know, Mr. Stuart, a woman is never expected to pay her bets.

Stuart. There's one woman who will pay hers to me, and that promptly. Attention, please. As a forfeit, you are to say to me, "I love you."

Mrs. V. T. Ah, Mr. Stuart, don't make me tell any more untruths!

Stuart (taking her hand). Don't say it then; tell me without words.

[*Stoops head and they kiss. Sounds of altercation outside.*
Agnes (coming down with Fred*).* What's that?

Charlie *and* Reg. *enter at b. d. and come down.*

Charlie. Well, you reprethentative of a graveyard, you juth athk her.

Reg. Ask her? I tell you she's engaged to me. (*Sees Stuart*). Aw, Mr. Stuart, you've lost your wager.

Stuart (to Agnes). Has Mr. Van Tromp proposed to you this evening?

Agnes. No.

Charlie (reeling with laughter against mantel). Ha, ha, ha, ha, ha! Oh, thith ith rich! Oh, I thall die of laughing! Oh, thum one thtop me! To think of the proud and haughty Reginald De Lanthy Van Tromp propothing to the wrong girl, — ha, ha, ha, ho, ho, ho!

Stuart. Laugh away, Newbank. Get it all in now, for it won't last.

Charlie. Won't latht? I don't under-thtand you.

> [POLLY, *with domino on her arm,*
> *appears at b. d. — looks in, and*
> *starts back as if frightened.*

Agnes. Come here, Polly.

> [POLLY *comes down r. between*
> CHARLIE *and* REG.

Stuart. Here is the minx who can make all clear. Polly, did Mr. Newbank propose to you?

Polly. Yes, sir.

Reg. Oh, deah, how funny! Haw, haw, haw! But then, people in his station always do take maids. Pwoposing to a servant!

Polly. But you proposed to me too, Mr. Van Tromp.

Charlie (*laughing very hard*). Holy Motheth, but I thall thertainly die of laughing!

Polly. Please, Miss Wortley, forgive me?

Stuart. Yes. Remember what she has done for (*points to Fred and Agnes*) you two.

Fred. And for (*pointing at Stuart and Mrs. V. T.*) those two.

Agnes. But she must have a lesson.

Stuart. Why, we 've all had a lesson — on the mysterious means Cupid employs to accomplish his purposes.

Mrs. V. T. Verily 't is so:

> " Love goes by haps,
> Some Cupid kills with arrows, some with traps."

CURTAIN